DANNY ORLIS
AND
DOUG'S BIG DISAPPOINTMENT

DANNY ORLIS

AND

DOUG'S BIG DISAPPOINTMENT

BERNARD PALMER

Danny Orlis and Doug's Big Disappointment
© 2024 by Bernard Palmer
All rights reserved. First edition 1973.
Second edition 2024.

Cover image: Adobe Firefly
Character illustrations: John Ball
Editor: Ruth Clark

Aneko Press Youth

www.anekopress.com

Aneko Press, Life Sentence Publishing, and our logos are trademarks of Life Sentence Publishing, Inc.
203 E. Birch Street
P.O. Box 652
Abbotsford, WI 54405

JUVENILE FICTION / Religious / Christian / Action & Adventure

Paperback ISBN: 979-8-88936-082-7

eBook ISBN: 979-8-88936-083-4

10 9 8 7 6 5 4 3 2 1

Available where books are sold

CONTENTS

CHAPTER 1

LONESOME

DeeDee Davis stood at her locker, her arms loaded with books. A deep longing took hold of her as she listened to the excited confusion of voices all around her. There was a game that night and the exhilaration of the pep rally that had just ended still excited the kids in the halls. Tina Nicholson, the girl who lived next door, hurried past with two or three friends in pep club uniforms, but they were so busy with their own plans for the evening that they didn't even see DeeDee, who longed for just one real friend in her new school.

She was still immobile, fighting her own loneliness, when a familiar figure rounded the corner and approached slowly. DeeDee recognized Letitia Warren from church, and a faint smile almost overcame her frown. Letitia had not seemed friendly when they had been introduced at the youth meeting a week or so before, but that was completely forgotten now.

Letitia hesitated as she passed DeeDee's locker. She seemed about to speak. DeeDee shifted her books expectantly from one arm to the other. They both lived in the same general direction from school. Letitia was probably going to suggest that they walk home together, DeeDee supposed. If she didn't, DeeDee decided to suggest it herself. At least it would be a beginning toward getting acquainted with some of the girls in her class.

"Hi, Letitia," DeeDee called out over the clamor in the hall.

The other girl paused and answered the greeting with a melancholy, "Hello." Then, without stopping she turned her head and pushed through the crowd, leaving DeeDee standing alone.

DeeDee lowered her gaze quickly, afraid someone would see the tears glimmering there. Letitia did not want to be her friend. Nobody in Rock Point did!

Mechanically, she propelled herself toward a side door. She was caught up in the surge of kids and was moved forward by them, but she was not a part of the gang. She was like a stick floating in the river, a piece of debris that did not mean much to anybody.

That was the trouble, DeeDee told herself. She simply did not belong in Rock Point's Northwest High. She and her triplet brothers, Del and Doug, had been going to school there since they had moved to Colorado from Minnesota with their foster parents; but actually, she was not a part of it. She went to classes, the library, and the games. That was all.

Once outside the building, she trudged wearily across the parking lot to the street that led to their home. Other kids were walking together in twos and threes, laughing and talking the way she and Sandy Cole and Brenda Ekberg used to do back in Fairview, but nobody spoke to her. It was almost as though she was invisible to them, for all the interest they showed in her. Nobody really cared whether she was around or not, DeeDee decided.

It had been that way ever since she and the boys moved to Colorado with Danny and Kay Orlis from their former home. She had gotten acquainted with a few of the kids at church and one or two at school, but she could not say she had a real friend anywhere in Rock Point.

She had met Letitia Warren and for a moment, she thought she was going to have a chance to get better acquainted with her. That had not worked out, however. Letitia had scarcely spoken to her.

DeeDee had wondered about the Warren girl the first time they met. She seemed so aloof and so unhappy. If she were new in Rock Point, DeeDee would have been able to understand it. She felt the same way herself most of the time. But Letitia had lived in the area most of her life. She should have known scads of kids.

DeeDee had been so disturbed by Letitia's coldness that she asked her brothers what they knew about her.

"She's OK, I guess," Doug said, "but she's sort of weird. She acts as though she's carrying the whole world on her back."

DeeDee agreed with him, but that only made her the more curious. "Has her brother Hank said anything about her?"

Del shook his head. "No, but if we go over to their house, she disappears. I don't think she wants to be around anyone."

After talking to her brothers, DeeDee was more concerned than ever about Letitia, and for a couple of nights or so she prayed for her. That soon stopped, however. Her own problems seemed more pressing than Letitia's.

As DeeDee walked home alone day after day, she thought about the few kids she knew at Rock Point. Tina Nicholson was friendly enough, especially now that she and Doug were beginning to get interested in each other. But most of the time, she was so busy she acted as though she did not even know DeeDee.

Hank Warren was OK, but he was certainly no one special to her. He came around the house once in a while and she had talked with him for a few minutes, but that was all. He didn't seem to be the kind of person she would want for a close friend.

And those were the kids she knew best. She didn't have a real friend in Rock Point and probably never would have.

Back in Fairview she had been busy all the time. She was in the pep club, sang in the girls' sextet and chorus, and had a part in the school play. She had played well in the flute section of the band and was vice president of her class. There had been parties to go to in Fairview, but at Rock Point she was not even invited.

There were things going on at the church they attended in Rock Point, but most of the time DeeDee did not feel like going. It was no fun because she had no close friends; and so she spent her time sitting in a corner or standing on the fringe of things, wanting to join in, but afraid to.

DeeDee wrote often to her friends back in Fairview, especially to Sandy and Brenda, and waited eagerly for their letters. School and church there were as exciting as ever. Fairview's football team had had a perfect season, and their basketball squad had lost only two games. Everyone was excited about the musical that was to be given in a couple of weeks, and the seniors had started practicing for their class play. Sandy had the lead and wrote that there was a part in it that would have been exactly right for DeeDee.

"Even Miss Martin says it is a part that's made for you. Oh, DeeDee, there are so many times when I can hardly stand to think of you being so far away. We'd have a ball this year if you were only here to be with us."

DeeDee tried to choke back her tears as she read. She felt as badly about being away from Fairview as Sandy did about her not being there.

If they had only stayed there, she reasoned, she would have had the part in the play. But the play was only one of the things she missed out on. At Fairview she would have been in so many other things that she never would have had time to be lonely.

But that was not all that was bothering her at this particular time. The gang in Fairview would be having a whole round of Christmas parties. Sandy had written about those, too, and asked her if she could come back to visit.

"I talked with Mother about it," she had written, "and she said I can ask you to come and visit us for Christmas. You've got to come, DeeDee! You'll be the only one of our whole gang who won't be here!"

At first DeeDee prayed about it hopefully, thinking there might be a chance for her to make the trip. She knew, however, that it would do no good to ask. There was never money enough around the Orlis home for a trip like that. Besides, Danny had strong ideas about everybody being home for Christmas. He would never let her go back to Fairview at that time of year, no matter how homesick she was. It would be best to just forget the whole thing. Only it wasn't quite that easy.

Whenever DeeDee felt homesick, which was almost all the time, she would think, *if only Danny hadn't been offered that job as instructor in the new mission flight school, or if he hadn't taken it! Everything would be so different then.*

As she felt more and more sorry for herself, she would grumble inwardly, *if he was so sure moving to Rock Point was the Lord's will for him, why didn't Danny move and let Kay stay in Fairview with Doug and Del and me so we could finish school with our friends?*

But almost as soon as she thought it, she realized how silly she was. She knew she had agreed to go. In fact, there were certain things about the change to Colorado that had intrigued her, but that had been because she wasn't aware of the loneliness that she would face or the problems in getting acquainted.

One afternoon on the way home from school DeeDee thought, *if only our own parents had lived, they would have been more considerate of the way we kids feel. They would have cared about the fact that we didn't want to leave our friends and move to a strange town while we were still in high school.*

She stumbled across the street and up the last half block to the house, her dark eyes almost blinded by tears.

Why had everything bad had to happen to her and her brothers? All the other kids that she knew had both of their parents and got to go to the same school, at least through high school. Parents who loved their children would never think of forcing them to change. They wanted them to be with their friends.

Her folks had been serving God out in Guatemala when they both drowned. She had never been able to understand that, either. They had given their lives to serve Him. Why hadn't He protected them? It wasn't that she didn't trust God to do what was best. She just didn't understand.

And after the terrible accident, she and Doug and Del had been sent to Fairview to live with Danny and Kay Orlis instead of living with their own relatives. Maybe if they could have stayed with Uncle Clarence and Aunt Carmen Roper at least they would have had someone looking after them who really cared about them.

Deep within, DeeDee knew she was being unfair with Danny and Kay, but her own self-pity was so great at the moment that she was unreasonable. All she could think of was that she had suffered so greatly because her parents had been missionaries.

Kay was sitting on the sofa reading a book when DeeDee opened the front door and came in.

"Hello, DeeDee," she said, pleasantly. "You're home early this afternoon."

"I'm home early every afternoon!" she blurted out bitterly. "Why shouldn't I be home early? There's nothing to do in this terrible place!"

Before Kay could speak, DeeDee stormed into her room and slammed the door. She knew it was not Kay's fault that she was lonely, but the hurt inside was so great right then that she had to blame somebody. She threw herself across the bed, muffling her sobs in her pillow.

Putting aside her book, Kay listened intently. She thought about going in to talk with DeeDee, and even got to her feet and started toward the door before she changed her mind. There was so little she could do or say to help her.

Silently she bowed her head and prayed for her young daughter. She had seen the ache in DeeDee's eyes the past few weeks and had noticed that she spent so much time alone. DeeDee never talked with her about it, but she knew her well enough to sense what was troubling her.

"It isn't like her to spend all of her time alone, the way she's been doing since we moved here," Kay told Danny when he came in from the airport just before dinner.

"She can't go around feeling sorry for herself. She's got to make an effort to make friends here, the way she did when she and the boys came to Fairview to live with us," Danny commented.

Kay was more understanding. "I know what she's going through. It was the same for me when I came up to Cedarton to go to school."

"I know it's hard on her," he replied, "but there isn't much that we can do to make it any easier for her."

In the bedroom DeeDee sat up and wiped her eyes. She just did not know what had been the matter with her lately. How could she really believe those things she had been thinking about Danny and Kay? She knew they loved her and the boys as much as their own parents could have loved them.

And she regretted the way she had spoken to Kay. She had had to leave her friends from Fairview just as DeeDee did. And Danny was not at fault. He had taken the new responsibility because he was sure God was calling him to it. He and Kay had always considered the triplets when they made their plans.

Slowly, she sat up and reached for her Bible. She had been reading a portion every day for the last several years, but for some reason the verses she read that afternoon had new meaning for her. When she finished reading, she prayed for friends, but even as she prayed, she doubted that she would ever again have friends like those in Fairview. The kids she had met since they moved to Rock Point did not seem to want her for a friend. They already had their own little cliques. Even the kids at church had their own friends and were too busy to have time to get acquainted with someone new.

She was still reading when Kay knocked lightly on the door and asked if she could come in. DeeDee hesitated. She was reluctant to have Kay come in just then, but there was no way to avoid it. She opened the door and Kay entered. Neither of them spoke at first.

Then Kay said sympathetically, "I wish there was something I could do to help you, DeeDee."

DeeDee threw her arms around her. She was so glad to be reassured of Kay's love.

CHAPTER 2

CHRISTMAS BREAK

Del and Doug Davis did not have the difficulty in making friends at Rock Point that their sister, DeeDee, was having. Being out for basketball helped them get to know quite a few guys. And they had each other for company, which made a great deal of difference.

Doug, however, had been wondering if that brother of his was always such an asset, especially when he wanted to eat lunch with Tina Nicholson, their neighbor. At a time like that, he would just as soon have shipped Del off to Africa or sent him on the first rocket ship to the moon.

He could get away from Del, but it was not quite as simple as it should have been. Just telling him he was going to eat with Tina was not enough.

"Oh, that's all right," he would say. "I like little Miss Cadillac's company, and I think she secretly likes me. Did you ever see how she looks at me when she thinks you're not watching?"

"Go on!" Doug growled. "Get lost!"

Del made his smile disappear and his lower lip trembled. "Is that any way to treat the only brother you've got?"

That was not all the ribbing he did, either. He would stay with them the whole time, even trying to sit between them if he got the chance. And he always monopolized the conversation. The only way Doug could put a stop to Del's corny tricks was to slip away from him, and he soon developed a whole battery of ways to do so.

Del always found out he had been deceived. By that time, however, Doug and Tina were usually through the lunch line and were at a table so surrounded by other kids so that he couldn't get within twenty feet of them. When that happened, he stormed around, grumbling that he had waited for Doug for so long that the food was all gone and he would only get half enough to eat.

"What do you expect me to do, cry about it?" Doug asked one evening.

"You could show a little brotherly concern." Del pretended to pout.

"Don't expect any sympathy from me," Doug said. "You're getting exactly what you deserve."

Doug was finding it easier to talk with Tina than when they first started seeing each other. He chatted with her in the hall and occasionally carried her books out to her car for her. The times he enjoyed as much as any were the lunches they so often ate together.

On one particular occasion, about a week before school dismissed for the Christmas holidays, he guided her to a table in the corner farthest from the door. Del came in some time later, but it seemed he could not find his brother or else he had given up heckling them.

Doug asked Tina about the English theme that was due on Friday and how she did on the history quiz. She was curious about the basketball team and whether he would be playing with the varsity. The subject was not one he cared to pursue at the moment. He did not know whether he was going to get back with the first string or not. As soon as he could, he started talking about the brief vacation they would be having.

"And where are you going to be for Christmas?" he asked.

Her smile flashed. "We never go anywhere at Christmastime. My grandma comes out from Denver and we all get together at our house to open our gifts on Christmas Eve and have a big dinner the next day."

"Sometimes we go back to Angle Inlet, Minnesota, where Danny's folks live, but I guess the whole family will be out here this year – Ron and his family and Jim and Connie Morgan and Uncle Carl and Aunt Mary Orlis – everybody."

"That's the kind of a Christmas I like," Tina said, "with lots of people around."

"Me too." It seemed to him as though they enjoyed most of the same things.

Doug enjoyed talking with her so much that soon he was sorry when they finished eating and the time came for them to go.

"I'm glad we live close enough to see each other during vacation," he told her.

There was a warmth and friendliness in the way she looked at him. "And we'll see each other at the youth retreat next week."

Youth retreat? Doug groaned inwardly. He had been upset about it ever since he first heard what they were planning. It was really going to be a skiing retreat and he still could not tell a schuss from a cloud in the sky.

"That's right." His voice revealed his lack of enthusiasm.

"You're going, aren't you?" she asked.

"Oh, sure." He tried to sound excited about the prospect, but he was unsuccessful. "Oh, sure, I wouldn't miss it."

"Neither would I." Her eyes shone. "It's the best retreat of the year. I just adore skiing, don't you?"

Doug flinched. He sure would love to ski, he told himself, grimly. He would love to have someone teach him so he could ski without breaking his neck and making a fool of himself.

Doug said nothing, but Tina continued to talk about the wonderful ski retreat they would be having. With something akin to horror, he realized Tina would be expecting him to be at the retreat, and she was also assuming that he knew how to ski. He groaned inwardly. How had he managed to get himself into such a mess?

But the time for straightening out things had passed. She was already talking about something else. The harm had been done.

He really wanted to go to the retreat. It looked as though he had no choice about it. He was going to have to go unless he got lucky enough to get pneumonia or break a leg.

It did sound like a lot of fun. He had to admit that. If only he and Del could learn something about skiing – just enough to keep from killing themselves. He and Del had been out several Saturdays in a row, trying hard, but they had made very little progress.

Del was beginning to get concerned, too. When they discussed the retreat that evening in their room, he said, "I don't know about you, but I'm beginning to wonder whether we should risk it or not. I haven't even learned to carry my skis yet, to say nothing about putting them on and wearing them."

"Oh, I'm going," Doug said brashly. "I wouldn't miss it." Then, as he realized what he had said and how Del would twist it, the color began to glow in his cheeks.

"That's right. I'd completely forgotten. Little Miss Cadillac will be there, won't she?"

Doug scowled resentfully.

"I don't blame you for wanting to be there. I would, too, if I were in your place. She probably won't like it if you don't go."

"What makes you think Tina has anything to do with my wanting to go to the retreat?" Doug countered.

"She might not like it if you stay at home," Del continued as though his brother hadn't even spoken. "But she might not like it if you try to ski and fall down and break your neck, either. Did you ever think of that?"

Doug snorted. Sometimes his brother could be the most stupid character he knew. "You let me worry about falling down, OK?"

"I would, but I'm sort of worried about it for myself. To tell you the truth, it's a lot worse for me."

"Oh, sure. I suppose you bleed more than I do."

"It's not that. I wouldn't have anybody to sit with me and hold my hand if I got all busted up. I'd have to suffer all alone."

The corners of Doug's mouth twitched. "You're going to start suffering right now if you don't lay off. I'm warning you."

Del moved to another chair across the room, his voice serious, but merriment crinkling his face. "I'll tell you what you could do that might be a big help."

"I don't need any suggestions from you."

"You can get Tina to go with you and teach you. That would be real togetherness."

"When you get done and want me to laugh, let me know. I wouldn't want to ruin your day by missing the joke."

"Spoken like a true, loving brother," Del countered. "And just for that I've got some other news for you. I understand Tina's folks are going along to be sponsors. You don't suppose they're doing that to keep an eye on you two, do you?"

Doug got to his feet.

"Don't you ever think about anything else?"

"Don't you?" Del's laughter followed him as he left the room.

DeeDee was glad for the brief vacation from school. In a way she was even glad that Uncle Carl and Aunt Mary Orlis and the others had to leave for home on Monday. She had enjoyed being with them, especially Ron and Darlene and their bubbling little boys, but she did not think she could keep up the pretense of being happy any longer.

She had not had a good time that Christmas. In fact, it had been miserable. All she could think about was the round of parties that were going on back in Fairview. Sandy and her other friends would be having so much fun that they probably would not even think about her.

DeeDee spent more and more time with Kay because she seemed to understand about loneliness.

She had thought her foster mother would tell her that she had to grow up and face the disappointments of life. Instead, she told her about her own experience with homesickness.

"I know exactly what it's like to be a girl in a strange town and a different school," she began, her face growing thoughtful. "You know my mother is a missionary in Mexico. Well, when the time came for me to go to high school, she sent me up to Cedarton, Minnesota, where I only knew three or four people."

DeeDee remembered hearing Danny and Kay talk about being in the school in Cedarton together, but she had never realized that Kay had come there under almost exactly the same circumstances as she had come to Rock Point. Somehow, that made her feel a little better. Kay really did understand what it was like for her.

"I was never so homesick in my life. I've never told anyone else this, but I used to cry myself to sleep every night."

"You did? What did you do to get over it?"

"First, I kept busy. I forced myself to go where the kids were and to take part in the things they were doing," she said without hesitation.

"Even if you weren't interested?"

"I seldom was interested. It seemed to me that everything they did was dull, but I was as active as I could be at school and church. I tried to keep myself so busy that I wouldn't have time to think."

"Oh." DeeDee could not avoid showing her disappointment. She thought Kay would have a speedy recipe for happiness. Her suggestion sounded even more awful than loneliness. "But what did you do when you were as busy as you could be and you still were homesick?" she asked.

"That's the other thing that helped me. I depended on God in a way I had never depended on Him before." Kay paused, toying with the wedding ring on her finger. "This probably won't make it much easier for you now, DeeDee, but, looking back, I'm sure my loneliness and the dependence on the Lord that I learned through it, brought a real turning point in my life."

DeeDee needed to be convinced that what Kay said was realistic. It was easy enough to say something but putting it into practice was something else. She really needed friends and nothing else drew her interest.

Still, it was encouraging to know that Kay understood how she felt. DeeDee would not have to bear her problem alone any longer.

Del and Doug were both concerned about the retreat because they did not know how to ski. As it developed, they had worried unnecessarily. By the time they pulled into the yard at camp, snow clogged the air and the temperature was dropping. The storm raged most of the time they were there and only let up some twelve or fifteen hours before it was time for them to go back to Rock Point. And when it did stop snowing, the wind continued to blow in strong gusts, making it impossible to get out on the ski runs.

The retreat was a failure as far as skiing was concerned, but spiritually, the three days were a tremendous success. The youth pastor presented a series of messages and discussions on personal commitment. The final evening service became a testimony meeting.

Thinking back on it, it seemed to Doug and Del that an important change in the retreat came when DeeDee got up and told how lonely she had been since moving to Rock Point. She asked for forgiveness from the kids in the group for the way she had felt toward them, for not giving them a chance to be her friends, and for blaming them for the way they treated her. She concluded by saying she was going to trust God to give her strength, encouragement, and victory.

The boys were surprised to hear her speak of the bitterness in her heart. They had not guessed that she was so unhappy.

When she finished, someone else told of a personal victory God had given her over a problem that had been plaguing her for the past several years. A boy asked for forgiveness for the way he had talked about the youth pastor and for pretending to live a Christian life when he was really doing just the opposite.

Another boy got up.

"I was brought up in the church, too," he said, "and I've been at all the meetings. If the speaker asked for some kind of a commitment – it didn't make any difference for what – I was the first up front. I don't know who I thought I was kidding, but I'd be feeling so proud of myself I felt like crying. And all the time I was a phony. The things I was saying and the things I've been doing when I thought no one was watching were completely different.

"I was just trying to make a big impression; to show people how good I was. Tonight, before God, I'm not doing that. I'm just saying that with His help things are going to be different in my life.

"I can't do it on my own, and I should know. I've tried it often enough. But I'm not going to depend on myself. I'm going to trust the Lord to guide me and help me each step of the way."

There were others. Many were challenged to a complete committal of their lives to Christ. Others told how they had confessed their sin and put their trust in Jesus for salvation.

It was one of the most wonderful meetings the Davis boys had ever been to. It lasted far longer than anyone had planned, and even then, the kids were reluctant to stop. In the boys' dorm later that night few were able to sleep. Several got together for a time of prayer. Others lay in their bunks talking with each other in guarded tones, or were motionless, talking silently to the Lord.

Of course, everyone hated to go home. Doug felt just like they did. After enjoying a spiritual uplift at the retreat, they had to return home and start school again. But it was like Danny said so often: if you are going to be useful to the Lord you have to get down to where people live and work with them. Staying in a separated place, even though it might be enjoyable, does not really help anyone. The battle for Christ is out in the world where those who are lost can be reached.

CHAPTER 3

LUNCHTIME DEVELOPMENTS

Basketball practice started with renewed fervor once vacation was over, but the coach was disturbed by the ragged play and poor timing of the first session of the new year and ordered scrimmages for the rest of the week.

"The way you guys are playing," the coach stormed, "I don't imagine one of you even thought about the team the past ten days. You probably didn't even touch a basketball. What did you do, spend all your time eating?"

He paused, looking over the squad coldly. "I'm going to work you so hard for the next few weeks that you'll be dragging. We're going to get the lard off and see you shaping up and sharpening up or you won't play basketball for me. Understand?"

Del knew they had gone into a slump, but he was more optimistic than the coach seemed to be at the moment. He'd only gained a couple of pounds himself, and he was sure Doug had as well. It wouldn't take long to sweat that off. He wanted to tell the coach that, but he was probably in no mood to hear a team member's defense.

After a couple of lengthy practice sessions, the guys began to play better ball, and the coach shortened the next practice period. When Friday night came, he congratulated them on the way they had gotten back into shape.

Del and Doug were again suited up with the reserves. They both had expected that. They felt fortunate to be out there at all. They were not on the starting team, but they both put in a fair amount of time on the floor.

Doug chalked up eight points, including a couple from the free throw line, and played a sharp game of defense that held his man to a scant three points. Del did not score at all, but he played the boards with skill, picking off rebounds and guarding his man so closely that he could not score while Del was in.

The coach said almost nothing about the way they played. No one had expected him to. Doug and Del were glad for the fact that he let them log some time. They were surprised when he patted them both on the back at the close of the game.

Danny, who was in the crowd, complimented them on the way home after the varsity squeaked by with a razor-thin victory. "I was proud of both of you tonight," he said. "You played a good game."

"Sure," Doug said, "but it didn't help us very much. We're still on the second string."

"That's all right. The second team of a school like Northwest is tougher than a good many of the varsity teams around the state. I thought you played very well."

Del's gaze caught his brother's, knowingly. "You aren't the only one who's proud of Doug, Danny."

"What do you mean by that?" Doug demanded uneasily.

"Tina Nicholson's proud of him, too."

"Lay off, will you?"

"Oh, I'm so sorry. I wasn't supposed to tell anyone, was I?"

DeeDee snickered. Usually, she felt sorry for the one who was being teased, but on this particular day she could not keep from laughing.

"Now we've got a comedian in the family," Doug exploded.

"Don't get so jumpy about it!"

Doug did not know how he was supposed to manage that, but he asked no more questions. He knew that the more response Del got out of him the more he would keep teasing. As soon as possible, he changed the subject.

The first day of school after the holidays, Hank Warren sought out DeeDee. She had been introduced to him a few weeks before when he made one of his infrequent visits to the youth group. She really knew very little about him. He was just a guy in their class as far as she was concerned. But he said he wanted to talk to her and sounded as though it was very important. He found her in the hall that her homeroom opened from.

"I've been looking all over for you," he said.

"I just got here," she told him. She was a bit puzzled by his manner.

"To tell you the truth," he continued, "I haven't been around here too long myself." He glanced at his watch. "I've got to talk to you, but I'm afraid there isn't time now. How about eating lunch with me this noon?"

She hesitated, trying to remember which period she had lunch.

"Don't tell me that you found yourself a steady boyfriend over the holidays."

"Oh, no, it's nothing like that. I just had to remember when I'm scheduled for lunch on Mondays. I eat during the fifth period."

"Great, that's my lunchtime, too. I'll see you." Then he hurried off to homeroom because the bell had just rung.

DeeDee thought about Hank from time to time that morning, curious as to why he was looking for her. She wondered what he was really like, but she was certainly glad that he wasn't as cold as his sister, Letitia.

When fifth period came and they went to the lunchroom together, Hank did not seem to have anything in particular he wanted to talk to DeeDee about. He said nothing about taking her out. It seemed that he just wanted to visit. He asked her what she did over the weekend, and after a time he asked her about Fairview.

"Doug and Del tell me you had so many boys hanging around your house in Minnesota that they stumbled over them," he said. "They said Danny was always having to chase them away so he could have a chair to sit in."

"You're just making that up."

"Ask them yourself if you don't believe me. It's exactly what they said."

Her cheeks colored delicately. She still could not believe her brothers said that. They never said things like that.

"I don't have to ask Del and Doug," she replied. "I already know."

The conversation drifted to other things. He told her about the little trip he and his sister had taken with their parents during Christmas break and that they just got back to Rock Point in time for school. He mentioned a new girl he had become acquainted with, describing her in some detail.

"She sounds nice," DeeDee agreed.

"She's all right, I guess, but I don't get too excited about going out with her. Besides, she lives too far away for that. Who wants to drive a couple of hundred miles just to go with a girl?"

"Thank you."

"You know what I mean."

All afternoon DeeDee thought about Hank. She had no idea why he had wanted to talk to her. He had talked with her as though they were old friends. It made her wonder, more than ever, what it was all about.

Doug was still as interested in Tina Nicholson as he had ever been, but he didn't say much about her around home anymore because of Del's teasing.

He saw Tina in the corridors from time to time, though, and walked to class with her. If there was time, he stopped to chat with her for a few minutes and once in a while they had lunch together.

Doug enjoyed those days and wished they could do it more often, but he knew that would be asking for trouble with Del around all the time.

Nevertheless, he was with her as often as he had the chance and was looking forward to the time when the basketball season would be over so he could take her out occasionally. Usually, he did not enjoy being around girls. They were too much of a drag. But Tina was different. And, surprisingly enough, she seemed to enjoy being with him, too. There were a lot of other guys around who were a lot sharper than he was and had lots more money. It seemed to him that most of them wanted to take her out, but they never got the chance. That surprised him even more than the fact that she enjoyed being with him. He thought a girl like her would have a couple of dozen boyfriends.

Tina was as thrilled about the retreat as he and Del and DeeDee had been, and still talked excitedly about it if they were together more than a few minutes. Mr. Nicholson said it was the most exciting three days he had ever spent. Mrs. Nicholson had not wanted it to end either.

Doug had wished that they could all return to the camp, but what he really wished that they could regain was that close relationship with Christ and the fellowship they had experienced.

Then Tina mentioned the part of the retreat that Doug had dreaded. "But I was disappointed that we didn't get to do any skiing, weren't you?"

"Not exactly." He had not intended to say that. The words slipped out before he thought.

She eyed him curiously. "What's the matter, Doug?" she asked. "Don't you like to ski?"

"I'm crazy about skiing," he told her.

"Then why didn't you care if we didn't get to ski on our retreat?"

He fumbled numbly with the words that would tell her why he had not wanted to ski the week before. He wished he could change the subject and direct her attention to mountain climbing or deep-sea diving or being lost in the desert – anything except skiing. But he had already said too much. There was no way to know how the blunt truth might affect their relationship, but there was nothing else to say.

"I've just never learned to ski, that's all."

She could scarcely believe it. The look in her eyes told him that such a shortcoming was unbelievable and almost inexcusable.

"You haven't learned to ski?" she echoed in a shrill voice. "I thought everybody knew how," she added disappointedly.

"Not Del and me. We've never lived where we had much of a chance to ski, so we haven't learned." He studied her shocked face helplessly. "But both Del and I are going to. I even bought a book about it."

"What?" Her forehead crinkled.

"I bought a paperback book that tells how to ski," he explained desperately. "Paid a whole buck for it. It's supposed to tell you everything there is to know about skiing. Del and I are going to learn or break our necks trying."

"You can't learn to ski from a book," she told him.

"You've never seen this book. It tells all about that fancy stuff like schussing and falling. That's what we're working on now – falling. We're getting pretty good at it, too. One of these days we'll break an arm or a leg, we're getting so good at it."

"You surely aren't serious," Tina said between giggles.

"I'll bring the book tomorrow and show it to you. I tell you, it's a wonderful book. It's got one whole chapter on using your head. I used my head even before I read the chapter, though. I slid down a hill on it."

Tears streamed from Tina's eyes and half the kids in that part of the lunchroom were trying to hear what Doug was saying.

"I see I'm going to have to help you learn to ski," she said, laughing, "or you are going to break something!"

"Del said I should get you to help me," he continued. "He said I should get you to hold the book and read it to me while I practiced doing what it said."

"I think maybe we'll forget the book. Seriously, Daddy has a cabin in the hills near one of the better known ski slopes and our family goes up there all the time to ski and ride our snowmobiles. Would you like to go along one of these Saturdays and learn to ski?"

Doug's eyes looked brighter. "You say you've got a snowmobile?"

"Two of them."

"You bet I'd like to come up; if it would be all right with your parents, that is."

"Oh, it's all right with them." Tina spoke confidently. "I can invite anyone from church I want to, as long as we don't have other guests, so there's room."

Going up to the Nicholsons' cabin with Tina's family sounded great, and especially the part about the snowmobiles. Doug had only ridden one a couple of times, but it had sure been a lot of fun.

"You can count on me any time there's room for a guest," he blurted. Then he checked himself and tried not to sound so exuberant. "I sure think it would be great."

"I think it would be a lot of fun. I'll talk with Daddy tonight and let you know when we'll be going."

Afterward, Doug wished he had thought to ask her if it would be all right to bring Del along, too. His brother was as anxious to ski as he was. He hated to have to leave him home. But he had been so excited when she gave him an invitation that he did not think about Del or DeeDee or anyone else.

Now it was too late. The conversation went on to other things, and if he mentioned it again it would look as if going skiing and snowmobiling with them was more important than anything else. Besides, there might not be room for anyone else. After all, it was good of Tina to invite him. He could scarcely ask her to take his brother along, too.

The only thing he could do was learn to ski himself, and then teach Del. Once he thought of that he felt a little better about leaving Del at home.

The next day Tina sought Doug out in the halls and told him that her dad thought it would be all right for them to take him along the next time they went into the hills.

"He said that as far as he knows, we'll be going up

to the cabin next Saturday morning, and you can go along then. How does that sound to you?"

"It sounds great," he said. "Absolutely wonderful."

"He also said you should bring your book along." Tina's eyes twinkled. "He doesn't know whether we'll be able to teach you without it."

"I think I'll give the book to Del. How about that?"

"Well, if you think you can spare it, I suppose it will be all right."

CHAPTER 4

DOUG FINALLY LEARNS

DeeDee and Hank continued their unusual friendship. Hank would frequently ask DeeDee to eat lunch with him, but he did not seem particularly interested in dating her.

One day at lunch, though, Hank warned DeeDee about being careful who she dated. She became indignant. Imagine him telling her to be careful who she dated, as though she were a little girl! He was just like her brothers.

"You don't have to tell me who to date. I can take care of myself without you or my brothers," she snapped.

"OK, OK," Hank answered, trying to calm her down. "Don't get angry. It's just that there are some guys around here who seem really great, but your brothers and I know that they're the wrong people to date."

DeeDee realized that Hank was really concerned and wanted to help. She softened her voice and said, "As a matter of fact, I'm not interested in dating anyone right now, anyway."

She was really thinking to herself, *nobody is interested in going out with me anyway.* Back in Fairview she had been one of the most popular girls in the school. In Rock Point she was a nobody. The ache she had been trying to push aside came rushing back.

* * *

Doug wanted to tell Del that he had been invited to go up into the hills with Tina's family the following Saturday to learn how to ski. He knew he was going to have to do it sooner or later, but he kept putting it off.

Finally on Friday afternoon he could postpone it no longer. He and Del had been planning to give skiing another whirl that Saturday. He had to explain why he was not going to go with him.

"Well, what time tomorrow morning do we take your little book and go out for another ski lesson, Doug?" Del wanted to know.

He looked up. "Well, I've been wanting to talk to you about that."

The tone in Doug's voice was disturbing. "What do you mean?"

"I'm not going skiing with you tomorrow."

Del's forehead crinkled.

"Don't tell me you're giving up on that book of yours just when we're beginning to get the hang of it."

"That's not it. You see, I've got other plans for tomorrow, that's all."

Suspicion gleamed in Del's eyes. "Like going somewhere with Tina?" he asked.

"Yeh, I'm going skiing with Tina and her family."

"I'm hurt. I'm cut to the bone. My own brother has turned me down for a girl. I didn't think it would ever happen." Del could really be dramatic when he teased Doug.

"I couldn't help it."

"I know. I know. Every word of hers is your command." He was enjoying Doug's uneasiness. "And exactly where is she leading you this time?"

Doug had some difficulty in speaking, and amusement rested lightly on Del's handsome young features.

"We–we're going with her folks to their cabin in the hills. She and her dad are going to teach me to ski."

Del's face grew serious and his lips curled. "So, that's it. I'm all right to go skiing with as long as you haven't got somebody else to be with, but when you get a chance like this, it's different."

Doug searched for words to explain, but he could not think fast enough.

"Thanks, old buddy. Thanks a lot." With that Del hurried off. He was not jealous of Doug but was feeling left out and sorry for himself.

Doug tried to study in the few minutes remaining

before dinner that Friday evening. He had enough homework to get done, especially since he was going up to the Nicholson cabin the following day and would not have a chance to crack a book. In spite of his pressing need to study, it was useless to try to get his mind on English after the trouble he had just had with Del.

He understood exactly how his brother felt. He would probably feel the same way if the two of them had something planned and Del backed out of it because he had a chance to do the same thing with a girl.

At first, he thought of trying to find his brother and apologize, but he thought Del was too angry to listen anyway. Doug renewed his efforts to read his English book.

About a half hour later, Del came back into the room. He stood inside the door, a crooked little smile pulling up at one corner of his mouth.

Timidly he asked, "What are you doing?"

"I was trying to decide whether I should go and find you to tell you I'm sorry I pulled such a sneaky trick on you," Doug said. "I shouldn't have told Tina I'd go with her and her folks tomorrow when you and I had plans."

"Forget it." He waved his hand as though to dismiss the entire matter. "I'd probably have done the same thing, if I'd been in your place."

"Just the same, that's no way for brothers to treat

each other. Especially guys who are as close as you and I are."

Del's smile left, briefly. He confessed to Doug that he had not been mad because Doug was going someplace else on Saturday, but he was hurt because he had not been invited too. Then he added, "I was way out of line. Will you forgive me?"

"Sure, I will. It's all over. As far as I'm concerned, it never even happened."

They continued to talk for a few minutes, sharing how they felt about other things.

"There's one thing I want to tell you, Doug," Del said. "I tease you a lot about Tina, but she's a good Christian kid and I like her a lot. Sometimes I even wish she had a sister."

Doug grinned. "She does. She's twelve years old."

"That wasn't exactly the kind of sister I had in mind."

When the Davis boys went into the dining room for dinner in response to Kay's call, they both felt closer to each other than they had for months. Del was glad he had gone to Doug and had gotten things straightened out between them. It was a lot better that way than letting things build until they were really mad at each other.

The following morning Doug got his skis and went up to the Nicholson cabin in the mountains with Tina and her family. It had been a long time since he had had so much fun. It was a still, cloudless day. When they arrived, the snow was unmarred except for the tracks of deer, elk, and mountain goats.

With help from Tina and her dad, Doug soon found that it was easier than it had been when he and Del had tried to learn from the book. He was soon able to handle himself quite nicely.

He still felt clumsy and unsure of himself. He floundered around and rocked unsteadily, but the long, narrow slats started doing some of the things he wanted them to do. He felt confident that with another lesson or two and a lot of practice he would be able to ski with the guys who had skied since they could walk. He began to see why Tina and almost everyone else in Rock Point found skiing so exciting.

"This is great, Mr. Nicholson," he said, his ruddy features beaming. "I know now why your whole family likes skiing so much." He was really thinking about Tina when he spoke.

"It just takes a little practice," Mr. Nicholson replied.

Doug and Tina went down a gentle slope together. The first time or two she stayed close by, but as his awkwardness began to vanish, she moved a short distance away to a steeper slope. He watched her enviously as she made sideslips and christies with the skillful ease of a pro. She waited for him at the bottom.

"I don't think I'll ever be able to ski the way you do," he said.

"Oh, yes, you will. Actually, I'm not very good," she told him.

"Now, don't give me that. I just saw you."

"But there are so many things I can't do," she protested. "I've been practicing to get into the ski patrol, but I've never felt I would have a chance to pass the tests."

Doug was no judge of skiing ability, but Tina looked sharp to him. He realized, of course, that he could be somewhat prejudiced.

"You should take the tests," he told her. "You would probably surprise yourself."

"Maybe I will next year."

That afternoon Mr. Nicholson suggested they try the snowmobiles.

"I've only been on a snowmobile a couple of times," Doug said. "I don't know anything about them, except that they're great fun."

"If you've ever driven a car or a boat, you won't have any trouble with one of these. They're quite simple to operate."

Doug surveyed the powerful machine once more. "It sure looks like fun."

"Oh, it is," Tina broke in. "To tell you the truth, I like snowmobiling better than skiing."

Mr. Nicholson explained the operation of the snowmobile to Doug before he drove away. There were a few things a driver had to watch out for, Mr. Nicholson explained, things like rocks hiding in the snow, or tree stumps, or fallen logs. And a little closer to civilization, there were fences. But watching the path ahead and using common sense was all that was required to avoid anything like that.

Doug started out slowly at first, feeling his way, testing what he knew about driving against the demands of this new vehicle. As Tina's dad had said, there were no particular problems unique to the operation of a snowmobile. It was about the same as operating a boat with a steering wheel.

After a brief swing up the mountain and back, Tina got on the machine behind Doug, and they went racing off together. She laughed happily as they roared along, and she screamed as he lurched into a turn. But it was great fun.

Doug had enjoyed skiing, it was true, but he was fascinated by the snowmobile. He liked the dull, throaty roar of the engine, the surge of power and the bite of snow against his cheeks. He liked to race across the trackless drifts and see the forest animals scurry away.

Doug liked to swing around the curves so fast that for a breath-robbing second, he was afraid the machine would go over. Tina tightened her grip and screamed again. His grin widened. It was not only the speed he enjoyed. He liked to stop at places where they could look out so far that he thought the distance must be like God's eternity, going on and on without end. He liked the sudden hush when the engine was shut off and the absence of sound was almost deafening.

Reluctantly Doug and Tina headed back to the cabin when the sun began to go down. They knew they would soon be having dinner and then they would return to Rock Point.

Doug helped Mr. Nicholson load the machines onto the trailer and fasten them securely.

"I sure do appreciate your invitation to come along today, Mr. Nicholson. It's been great."

"I've enjoyed having you." Then his smile became broader and his eyes twinkled as he added, "I think we all enjoyed your company."

Doug knew what he meant and colored slightly.

CHAPTER 5

CALL FOR HELP

DeeDee ate lunch with Hank Warren on the average of once or twice a week. Sometimes he walked her to class or met her at her locker for a brief visit.

Hank was really the only friend DeeDee had in Rock Point. She knew some other kids, but not well enough to confide in them, so she was still desperately lonely. She longed for another girlfriend she could confide in, someone like Sandy Cole who could share her secrets and pray with her. But it seemed too much to ask to ever have another friend like Sandy. DeeDee was resigned to never having any friends at all in Rock Point.

DeeDee could not bring herself to mention her homesickness to Hank. She could have told Sandy or another girl, but she kept it bottled inside, not daring to allow it to show.

However, she found her friendship with Hank

increasing to the point where she even sought him out on occasion, much as she would have sought out one of her brothers. When she had a problem in class or at home, she found she could talk with him, if the situation was not too personal. Hank seemed to feel he could do the same with her. It was no surprise to her when she found a note from him wedged into the crack between her locker door and the metal frame.

She read it, even though she knew what it said before she looked at it. That was Hank's standard way of getting in touch with her. The note said he wanted to have lunch with her that day.

"And it's important," he added.

She read it a second time, the frown lines in her forehead and around her firm mouth growing deeper. There was a different, more serious tone in this note, and she found it vaguely disturbing. It must be something more serious than anything else he had shared with her. There was a tone of urgency about it that she found vaguely disturbing.

DeeDee waited uneasily for lunchtime, and when it came, she hurried to their usual meeting place near the lunchroom door. Hank strode up to her with long, distance-eating steps a moment or two after she arrived.

"I see you found my note."

"How could I miss it?" she asked.

She hoped he would tell her what was so important immediately. Instead, he ushered her into the lunchroom. They got their trays and found a table in the far corner of the room where it was a little less crowded and noisy.

"Now," DeeDee began guardedly, just above a whisper, but with tension drawing her voice taut, "what did you want to see me about that's so terribly important, Hank?"

He grinned, "Now, wait a minute. Did I say it was important?"

"Yes, you did!" She was slightly annoyed. He was sounding like those brothers of hers again.

"I must have gotten carried away."

"Hank Warren, if that's the truth, I'm going to be mad at you for getting me all upset about nothing. I think I flunked a history quiz because of that note of yours."

He sipped his chocolate milk thoughtfully. "That's too bad. I didn't know it would affect you that way."

"What did you want to see me about?" she demanded. "Stop dawdling and tell me."

"Well," he began, "it's important, but I wouldn't say it's exactly critical, if you get what I mean."

She thought she understood, and she did feel relieved, but she could not let him know it.

"It's clear, all right," she replied. "The whole trouble is that I'm the one who's a little dense."

"I don't know that I'd say that." He went on, "You're a little silly, maybe, but not dense."

"Oh, thanks so much," she replied in a withering voice.

Hank would have answered her promptly, but a couple came up to the table nearest to them just then. He waited until they were seated and eating.

"You know my sister, Letitia, don't you?" he asked.

She nodded. She had met Letitia Warren at church and at youth group, but she thought she would never really get to know her. She had often wondered how there could be so much difference between a brother and sister. Hank was so exuberant and outgoing, so easy to get to know. Letitia was just the opposite. She was shy and quiet, the sort of girl who would sit alone at a party all evening unless someone took the initiative to go over and talk to her.

"She goes to our Sunday school," she said, "and I've seen her at some of our youth meetings."

"That's right. Letitia takes in everything at church, the whole bit."

"What's the problem?" she asked.

He sighed his concern.

"I don't even know for sure," he went on. "Maybe there isn't any problem. Maybe this is all my imagination, but Letitia bothers me, especially lately. She's so quiet now, and so withdrawn and introverted. She'd be happy just to sit and never say anything to anyone. Only she isn't really happy at all. It really bugs me."

"A lot of people are shy. I tend to be that way myself," DeeDee explained.

"I know that. But no matter how shy a person is, she should laugh once in a while, shouldn't she?"

"That is strange," DeeDee said. "I wonder why?"

"I wish I knew. It seems to me she blames herself for everything bad that happens around our place. Like last summer she blamed herself that we didn't go on a trip we'd planned because she got a bad virus infection. Mom and Dad had a touch of it, too, but she blamed herself. Sometimes I think she likes to feel sorry for herself."

DeeDee still was not entirely sure what the problem was, or what he thought she could do about it. She had difficulties of her own. How could she do anything for Letitia? But she did not tell Hank that. That was something a boy would not understand.

He was so concerned about his sister that he never noticed that she failed to answer his question.

"There's something else that gets me. Letitia doesn't have any friends. She walks to school alone and comes home alone and eats lunch alone. If you'll watch her, you'll see that she's never with anyone else. I don't know much about girls, but it seems to me that she should be with someone else once in a while."

DeeDee agreed with him. She knew what it was like not to have any friends. That was one of the things that bothered her most about Rock Point. The kids were so busy within their tight little cliques that she could not get a chance to get acquainted with them.

She felt like telling Hank not to blame Letitia for

not having friends. It was the town and the kids in school who were at fault. But she could not say anything to him about that without letting him know more about herself than she cared to.

"And what is it you'd like to have me do?" she asked reluctantly.

"I've noticed that you don't associate with too many other girls, either." He was almost apologetic. "I thought maybe you could make friends with her. Maybe it would help her, and you might enjoy having a friend, too."

"I'll do what I can." She wanted to sound more interested than she was, but her words came out flat and emotionless.

She thought that was all he wanted to talk with her about and was going to change the subject, but he still had not finished. "There's something else about Letitia that I thought maybe you might be able to help her with, if it's not too much trouble."

He was so pathetically concerned about his sister that she could not turn him down. "Of course, Hank. You know I'll do anything I can to help her."

"I thought you would." He breathed deeply. "She's built a shell around herself a foot thick. I've tried and tried to get through to her, but I can't. Maybe you can help her to see that life's worth living."

"I'll do what I can," she repeated. And this time she meant it.

Hank acted as though he had not heard her. His

gaze searched out some distant horizon far beyond the confines of the room they were in. His face hardened and there was a certain harshness in his voice.

"If that religion they preach over at that church of yours really means anything," he exploded suddenly, "why would they let a poor, lonely kid like Letitia come there Sunday after Sunday without trying to help her?"

DeeDee winced as the question drove its barbed shaft into her heart. Hank had not meant to accuse her. He was not even aware that he had hit her. He was talking about the kids who had been in the church and had known Letitia for years, and the adults who should have been more sensitive to his sister's needs.

However, DeeDee knew she was just as guilty as anybody else. She had seen Letitia in Sunday school and church every Sunday, sitting to one side with a lonely, wistful look clouding her face. Never once had she gone over and talked to her. Never once had she tried to help her, or even realized that she needed help. She had been concerned only with herself and the fact that she had no friends.

She saw now that she had been longing to get in with the popular kids at church and school, those who could help her to get into the center of activity where she used to be back in Fairview.

What was even worse, she had been so insensitive to the needs of the others around her that she had not been seriously disturbed by the fact that Hank was not a Christian. She had never prayed for him. She had not sought out an opportunity to witness to him. As far as she was concerned, she would let him go to a Christless eternity without caring. It was no wonder he had such a distorted view of the church and the gospel it preached.

"I'm afraid we're all guilty," she told him defensively. "We get so wrapped up in our own affairs that we never think about other people and the fact that they have problems, too."

Hank was somewhat embarrassed that she was applying his remarks personally. "I shouldn't have sounded off like that," he said. "I'm no better than anyone else. But when I see Letitia so lonely and disturbed and the people who could help her turning their backs on her, I get boiling mad. It looks to me as though all that piety they spout on Sunday doesn't mean too much."

"I know," she added weakly.

The lunch period was over, so the conversation ended. On the way out DeeDee turned to Hank once more. "I'll try to make friends with Letitia," she promised him, "but I don't know what success I'll have."

He thanked her for her concern. "I knew you'd want to help her," he said.

But did she really want to help Letitia? That question nagged at her the rest of the afternoon. Was she really concerned enough to try to help Hank's sister?

She could not say that she enjoyed being with a

quiet, sad-faced person who seldom laughed. Even if she did make friends with Letitia Warren, she would still be left out of things at Northwest High.

Everyone who was important at school would think of her as dull and uninteresting like Letitia if they saw the two of them together. She just might be ruining her own chances of ever getting to be anybody at Northwest High.

That, she realized, was a matter of pride. She wanted the kids at school to look up to her, to recognize her as somebody important. She knew that her pride was not glorifying to God. She was ashamed of her conceit and even more ashamed that it persisted.

If Letitia were an important individual in the eyes of the other kids at school, she would be eager to make friends with her. As it was, she wondered what Hank's sister would do to her chances of winning acceptance. Still, she had promised him she would try to help her. She had to try, regardless of what happened.

CHAPTER 6

DOUG PROVES HIMSELF

Nobody expected the basketball team to do very much that year. They had lost most of the first string by graduation the previous year and had an uncertain crop of reserves to draw from. They won their first game, which was usually an easy one, and dropped the next two. That was supposed to be the pattern for the year, but they came surging back to knock off three in a row before losing to the conference leader by a single point in a triple overtime.

Interest around the community began to increase and the crowds improved noticeably. No one was talking about them as conference champions, or even getting to go to the state tourney in March, but they were playing well enough to keep their opponents from rating them a pushover. Anyone who made that mistake soon learned a lesson.

The second team did much better than the varsity, losing only two games in the first half of the season.

Not only were their victories impressive, but also the way they trounced their opposition. They beat their opponents so thoroughly that the games were uninteresting to all but the most rabid Northwest fans.

Doug Davis was the top scorer and one of the two best defensive men. Getting to play regularly, he continued to improve as the season progressed. It was inevitable that he would be moved up to the varsity before the year was over. Everybody was expecting it. Everybody, that is, except Del. He had not thought about it one way or the other. When it happened, however, he had to admit that Doug deserved it.

The change came at the close of the last practice before the Milford game. The head coach called both squads together to talk to them. He told them he was making some changes and explained why. By that time, although he mentioned no names, they were all aware of what was going to happen. At the close he read off the names of the starting five and the two who were demoted to the second string.

"And tomorrow night Doug Davis and Ed Bromley from the second team will be suited up with the varsity."

Del glanced quickly at his triplet brother. He was no longer angry with Doug because he could play basketball better than he could. That had been settled back in Fairview. Actually, he was glad for him. He worked hard and was easily the best player on the second team. He deserved a crack at the varsity. And he would make it, too, if he got half a break.

But Del's own feelings of inferiority and resentment came back to him. He never would have been able to do anything outstanding on the basketball court, but if they had only stayed in Fairview, he would have been the football star. He had earned that honor the year before, and he was heavier and faster now than he had been at that time. The people in town were talking about sweeping the conference and being named the state champs. All on the strength of his ball carrying. If he could have stayed in Fairview, he would have made a real name for himself. He even might have gotten a football scholarship to one of the big schools.

Things had not worked out that way, however. They had to move to a city where the school they attended was almost as big as the whole town of Fairview. Then, when they got there, Northwest had the best football team they had ever had, and he could not even get on the squad!

Del swallowed against the lump that came up in his throat. It seemed that no matter how hard he tried, he never got any breaks. He came out on the short end of everything.

Del kept his resentment from Doug. He knew he was not to blame.

"I wish you could move up to the first team, too," Doug said. "Then I'd really be happy."

"Forget it." He gestured his indifference. "You're the basketball player in the family. You should have moved up a long time ago. You're a lot better than most of the guys on the varsity."

"I wouldn't say that."

"I wouldn't, either," Del said, grinning. "I just wanted to make you feel good."

Doug was so happy that Del's teasing remarks did not even bother him. He could not even get angry when Del kidded him about Tina and how thrilled she must be now that her hero was on the varsity.

"She'll be so happy that you're out on the floor giving your all for dear old Northwest High. I can hear her now."

"Lay off, will you? You're just jealous because you don't have a girl like Tina."

"You can say that again. I really dig that Cadillac and the ski lessons and those snowmobiles of hers." For the first time bitterness crept into his voice.

Danny was excited about the fact that Doug had been moved to the varsity and for a while that night the whole family talked about it at the dinner table.

"I'm proud of you, Doug," Danny said. "You really accomplished something by getting on the first string in a school as large as Northwest. With so many fellows to choose from, the competition is bound to be rough."

"I still can't believe that it happened. I keep thinking it's a dream and I'll be back with the second team when I wake up."

"It's true, all right," DeeDee assured him so solemnly that they all laughed. "It's right here in the paper."

"I'll probably be back on the second team after tomorrow night's game," he said. "Just because I got moved up for one game doesn't mean that the coach will let me stay."

"Oh, you'll get to stay, all right." Del spoke up loyally. "You're as good as any of the other guys on the first string, that's for sure. And, as far as I'm concerned, you're better than most."

"You haven't been doing so bad yourself the last couple of games."

Del brushed a hand through his thick, dark hair. Doug didn't have to say that. He knew well enough that he didn't have it to make the varsity. He was pushing himself to stay where he was. He had thought he was going to get cut several weeks ago.

"Me?" he echoed aloud. "I'm lucky to hang in there with the reserves."

"You might surprise yourself next year," Danny commented.

Del squinted across the table at Danny. At first, he thought their foster father was kidding him, but he was completely serious.

"This is really your first experience playing

basketball since you've been in high school. That can make a big difference. I've seen a lot of improvement in your playing since the season started. Unless I'm badly fooled, you'll be up with the others next winter."

Del could not agree. He had to admit he was out of any sport when it came to Northwest. There were too many top-notch guys around.

"Maybe," he said aloud, and without conviction. It would just be his luck not to get to play at all next year. That was the way things were happening to him lately.

Del decided not to even go out for the team next year. It was bad enough to be a junior on the reserve team, but he was determined not to be stuck there as a senior.

The following night Northwest played Milford. With Doug out of the reserves lineup, the coach made some changes. He moved Del to forward and played him most of the game. That was a pleasant surprise to him. He thought he would be riding the bench most of the time.

Del lacked the finesse of his brother. That was obvious to practically everyone in the stands, but he played well. He had a certain rough skill about him, a drive that was thrilling to watch. When he went off the floor, he was given a round of applause.

The Northwest reserves won the game by a scant six points, and the coach had a word of commendation for Del.

"You really came through for us tonight, Davis."
His smile flashed. "Thanks."

"Next year you'll be giving that brother of yours a run for his position."

Del showered and dressed thoughtfully. That was something unexpected. He never thought the coach would say anything like that to him. It had happened twice in the last two days. He began to wonder if what they were saying was really true. It would sure be a switch if it was. Doug would be more surprised than anyone. He always assumed that he was the better basketball player of the two.

Although Doug suited up with the varsity, the coach stayed with his regulars most of the first quarter and half of the second. It was not until one of the starting forwards picked up two personal fouls in as many minutes that he sent Doug in.

"Fake that guard out, Davis," he said, "and drive in close for a layup. You'll be wide open."

Doug nodded anxiously.

At the moment he was so excited, he was not even sure he could hang on to the ball or find the basket if he did. His whole future on the team was riding on the next few minutes. If he were able to get hold of himself and play the way he had with the second string, he would be in solid. If he was not successful, the chances were that he would be back with the reserves. He trotted stiffly out onto the floor and took his position.

Northwest built up an early lead, but in the last three or four minutes Milford got hot and was pressing hard. They took the ball in just beyond the center line and began to move it forward, passing it from one guard to the other in a measured pattern, while the forwards and center shuttled in and out.

A signal from the captain and the ball was rifled to one forward, who slammed it to the hard driving center. He faked to his right and looped the ball in for a basket which tied the score.

Northwest took the ball and worked it forward calmly. There was still plenty of time left in the first half, and they had all of the second half before them. There was no need to get nervous. An orderly, well-planned attack was always better, their coach preached. Let the opposition get tense and flustered. They should stay cool and play a calculated game. They would always do better. That was the one outstanding characteristic of the Northwest basketball teams.

Doug could have played that sort of game himself, had he not been so nervous, so eager to make good. He was always cool with the reserves. The first time he got the ball with the varsity, however, he was so excited he threw it away. The next time he double dribbled and lost it to Milford.

Northwest took time out at a signal from the coach, and the team went over to where he was standing. He spoke to Doug reprovingly. "You're all shook up.

You've got to get hold of yourself, or you'll do more good for Milford than you will for us."

"I'm all right now." He was afraid he was going to be taken out.

"You're doing fine. Just settle down and play ball. We're not beaten yet, and we're not going to be. Just remember that."

When play resumed, things went better for Doug. He knew he would not be taken out, at least for a while. That gave him enough self-confidence to relax and start playing ball the way he had with the reserves. He was far from being the star, but he played an acceptable game. When the final gun sounded, Northwest had chalked up another victory with a comfortable lead.

Del waited in the hall outside the locker room for his brother to come out. He just wanted to talk to Doug in private for a minute before he went off to the church party with Tina. That was the way it was lately. Del had always had Doug's company but now he spent time with DeeDee.

CHAPTER 7

TO BEFRIEND AN ICEBERG

DeeDee wished desperately that she had never promised Hank that she would try to befriend his sister and help her with her problems. She was sure there was nothing she could do for anyone. She had too many difficulties of her own. But she gave him her word, and she knew he would be asking how she was doing with Letitia. She had to try.

Even before she started, she knew that getting acquainted with the other girl would not be easy. Letitia never spoke to anyone unless she had to. She would nod or shake her head, and on rare occasions manage a sad, twisted little smile.

It was the same in class. She never volunteered to answer a question, and there were times when it seemed that she avoided answering questions put to her directly because she was afraid to speak.

DeeDee tried to work out a casual approach to

get better acquainted with Letitia. She contrived to walk with her between classes, but Letitia practically refused to talk to her.

"That history quiz was horrible, wasn't it?" DeeDee began.

Letitia nodded.

"I made an awful mistake studying for it. I got fouled up and studied the wrong chapter."

Her companion acted as though she had not even heard her.

DeeDee tried again. "Does Miss Simpson always assign so much homework?"

"I don't know." She spoke so softly DeeDee could scarcely hear her.

She had never met anyone like Hank's sister. Letitia was not shy. She was antisocial. She seemed glad when they reached the room where she had her next class, so she could avoid any possibility of conversation.

DeeDee could not imagine trying to push herself onto the other girl again. It did no good. Letitia had no friends because she wanted it that way. It was as simple as that. Still, Hank was so concerned about his sister and was so anxious for DeeDee to make friends with her that she had to keep trying.

On Tuesday and Friday she waited in the hall outside the lunchroom until Letitia came along because they had the same lunch period then.

"Hi, Letitia," DeeDee exclaimed as warmly as she could. "How are you?"

She smiled and nodded in greeting, but that was all.

"I've been waiting for you. Would you like to have lunch with me?"

The sad-faced girl hesitated so long that DeeDee was afraid she was going to be turned down. Letitia surprised her. "I think I'd like that," she said at last.

They got their food and found a table. Letitia started to eat immediately and seemed embarrassed when DeeDee bowed her head and returned thanks.

Letitia seemed to like her well enough. She seemed to appreciate that DeeDee had suggested they eat together, and she answered her questions when she asked them. But she initiated no conversation on her own and seldom said anything more than was absolutely necessary. Her facial expression seldom changed, except to become a bit more forlorn and sad. It seemed to make no difference whether DeeDee was there or not. She still wore that same dour mask, as though to hide any feelings within.

DeeDee talked to Kay about Letitia.

"I don't know what's the matter with her. When I'm talking to her, I get the impression she'd prefer I go away and leave her alone. She acts as though she doesn't really want any friends."

"She's probably so shy she's embarrassed to talk to you," Kay replied. "I'm sure she doesn't really feel that way."

DeeDee could not believe Kay's theory. She had tried talking with Letitia enough to know that her problem was more than shyness. Sometimes she thought Letitia liked her. On other occasions she was not so sure. She decided that it just would not be worthwhile to try many more times. All her friendliness was being wasted.

DeeDee invited Letitia to go to the church party following the Milford basketball game, but she acted as though she disliked parties.

"I went to the last one," she protested, "but I didn't have any fun."

DeeDee had not been to a party since moving to Rock Point, but she had never missed one when they lived in Fairview. "We used to have some wonderful parties where we used to live. Everybody says this one is going to be a blast."

Letitia's lips trembled. "Most of the parties I've been to are a bore."

DeeDee actually had not planned on going to the party herself, but, impulsively, she asked her new friend to go with her. "I just know that we could have a great time."

"I'll see." She spoke without enthusiasm. "I might go if I don't have anything else to do."

DeeDee was so convincing that she could hardly believe it herself. She just kept talking until Letitia agreed to go.

"Swell. I know you'll have a ball. We'll stop by for you. You can go to the game with us."

Hank was grateful for DeeDee's efforts to befriend his sister. "It might not mean much to you," he said, "but she hasn't gone to a game for the last couple of years. She wouldn't even go when I was playing football. This is great!"

A warm glow enveloped DeeDee. It had not been easy to get Letitia to agree to go to the party, but she had succeeded. Now, if only she had a good time! Maybe she would start going to the rest of the games that season and some of the other school activities.

An hour before they were to leave for the game, however, the phone rang. It was for DeeDee.

"This is Letitia Warren." Her voice sounded strained and taut. "I don't believe I can make it to the game and party tonight. I'm sorry."

DeeDee's hopes collapsed around her. Hank's sister had turned her down! And she had been counting so much on her!

She was so disappointed she no longer felt like going to the game herself. She would have stayed home if Danny had not reminded her that Doug was playing his first game with the varsity.

"There may not be another time to see Doug play varsity this season," Danny said. "He's on probation tonight. If he plays well enough, he'll get to stay. If he doesn't, he'll be sent back to the second team, and that would probably end it for this year, at least. We should be there and support him."

"If that's the way it is, I'll go," she said reluctantly. Her lips were trembling. "But I can tell you now that I don't feel like it." She turned to Kay. "What makes Letitia like she is, anyway?"

"I don't know for sure, but I know that the Lord has the answer to her problems. If she would only turn her life over to Jesus, He would give her the strength and courage she needs to get her problems straightened out."

DeeDee was sure her cheeks flushed. Kay spoke so confidently that she felt foolish for not relying on the Lord. DeeDee said nothing to Kay about it, but she thought how much she was like Letitia, miserable and unhappy most of the time. Kay would probably tell her the same as she had before that she should be putting her trust in Jesus to give her victory. But it seemed easier to say it than it was to do it.

If she had been able to succeed with Letitia, she might have developed confidence enough to completely trust God to solve her own problems. As it was, she thought she could never depend upon Him to work things out for her without trying to work things out herself. When they moved from Fairview her life had come apart.

In the weeks that followed DeeDee tried occasionally to make friends with Letitia Warren. There were times when she thought she was making progress.

Letitia surprised her on some occasions by laughing and joking the way the other kids did. That was not too often, however. Usually, she was cold and unresponsive. During those periods DeeDee was sure she was getting nowhere.

She talked with Hank apologetically about her feeling of failure.

"I'm beginning to think I'm wasting my time and hers," she said. "Letitia is so indifferent when I try to be friendly. I don't think she even likes me."

He spoke quickly. "Oh, she likes you, all right," he assured her. "She talks a lot about you around home. She considers you the best friend she's got."

"That's a surprise to me."

DeeDee began to wonder if Hank might not be stretching the truth about Letitia's attitude toward her in order to spare her feelings. But she decided that Hank would never do that. Although he was not a Christian, he was too honest to deceive her. He might remain silent in an effort to hold the truth from her, but he would never lie to her. She was sure of that.

"Hang in there, kid," he told her, "and don't give up. You'll get to Letitia sooner or later. You're making progress little by little."

Kay was more help to DeeDee than Hank had been. She seemed to understand much more about girls like Letitia than he did.

"What do you suppose makes her like she is?"

she asked Kay one evening when they were doing the dishes together.

"I've never met her, so I couldn't tell you why she's like she is. Even if I had met her, it's likely that I wouldn't know, but usually there's a reason."

"That's what I keep telling myself, but I'm not able to get close to her at all. Sometimes she's friendly and I begin to think she enjoys being with me, but other times she acts as though she hardly knows me and doesn't want me around. Lately I've had the feeling that she doesn't believe I really want to be her friend."

"Maybe she doesn't."

DeeDee stopped what she was doing and turned questioningly to Kay. "What do you mean?"

"I don't know whether I'm just making this up out of nothing, but I remember a friend of mine when I was going to school in Cedarton. At first, I had a terrible time getting close to her because she had confided something to a friend who proved to be untrustworthy. Maybe something like that happened to Letitia at one time and she doesn't want to trust anyone else because she's afraid of being hurt again."

DeeDee was not sure she understood all that Kay meant, but there had to be some reason for Letitia's attitude, that was certain. She was one of the strangest persons she had ever been around.

In a way she resented Letitia's unfriendliness. Why did she have to be so difficult? She had lived in Rock Point all her life. She should have known all the kids and had lots of important friends. DeeDee thought to herself how different things would have been if she had lived in Rock Point for three or four years.

Of all the kids in school it seemed that Hank Warren was about the only one she could count as a friend. They ate together in the lunchroom and talked for a few minutes whenever they met in the halls. Once in a while he gave her a ride home from school and they would sit out front in the car to talk. DeeDee shared some confidences, but she could not say everything she wanted to a boy.

DeeDee prayed that Hank would see his need to confess his sin and place the Lord Jesus Christ on the throne in his life. She even prayed that she might have an opportunity to witness to him. Lying awake at night, she would try to plan what to say to him.

It was not easy trying to talk to a guy like Hank about sin and his need to commit his life to Jesus Christ. He was not like the average fellow at Northwest. He did not smoke or drink and the girls he went out with all said he was a gentleman whenever they were with him.

One of the girls at school told DeeDee how she felt about him. "I'll take him over a lot of those Christian guys the people in your church think are so great. Go out with one of them and you find out they've got more arms than an octopus!"

DeeDee had never dated him, but she knew him to be considerate and thoughtful. She thought it would not be easy to get a person like him to see that he needed Jesus; that he had to confess his sin and trust Him for a new life. By human standards Hank was good enough. Still, she knew he had committed the biggest sin of all. He had rejected the claims of Jesus Christ on his life.

Although DeeDee waited for an opportunity to talk with Hank about his need of a personal relationship with Jesus, it had not come.

CHAPTER 8

DEL'S SLUMP

Doug had been concerned, at first, about consistently playing basketball well enough to remain on the varsity. He was sure that after a game or two he would start to slip, or one of the other guys would begin to improve enough to take his place and he would find himself back with the reserves. But it was not long until he was solidly established with the first string and was even getting to start occasionally.

In one way his promotion helped Del as far as getting to play more was concerned. The forward who was sent down from the varsity was so angry that he turned in his suit, which caused the coach to depend on Del in a way he had never done before. Del played most of the time in the next two or three games, being taken out only to rest briefly.

He seemed to play as well as ever, especially in the eyes of the crowd. There was a difference, however; a difference only he was aware of. He never had possessed Doug's fierce desire to win. Now he cared even less. He soon realized that he played because he enjoyed it. Whether or not he did an acceptable job did not matter much to him. If he scored a few baskets and mixed it up on defense, that was all that mattered. And, if they happened to win in the process, that was OK, too. He guessed he enjoyed winning, but he was not about to get upset if they lost. Lately Doug had asked him several times how he could keep his cool when the score was close.

"I sure don't see how you do it. You act as though you don't care whether you win or not."

Del laughed. "What good does it do to come all unglued over a basketball game?"

"I'd give anything to be like you are," Doug exclaimed. "When the score gets close or we're behind, I want to win so bad it's the only thing I can think about. I have to keep praying that I'll act like a Christian instead of fouling to keep the other team from scoring."

"What you need is to relax a little and don't let winning mean so much to you."

"Who can do that?"

"You asked me how to keep your cool. All you have to do is to quit thinking so much about what it's like to win. Me? I couldn't care less." Del's voice sounded proudly flippant.

"You're putting me on."

Del changed the subject. He knew his brother did not believe him. That was what made it so hard for Doug. He thought winning was so important. If that was the way he wanted it, Del thought, let him get high blood pressure and have a stroke or something. Del was determined not to get too excited about anything. Unfortunately, Del was beginning to notice that he had taken the same attitude toward his studies.

Del still took his books home every night, the same as ever, and at times he went into the bedroom to study. But something had happened in his attitude toward classes. If he got his papers finished and handed in when they were due, that was fine. If he felt like goofing off and being unprepared, that was OK too.

Right now, he had an English theme to write, an important one the teacher said, that had to be finished the following afternoon. He had been putting it off until now the deadline was approaching, and the work was only half done. He had not even completed all the research, and one of the books he needed was checked out by somebody else. He could never get it done on time now even if he sat up most of the night, and he was not about to do that. As far as he was concerned, anyone who stayed up most of the night to study was out of his skull.

Del got up from his desk and went to the window where he spent some time staring out into the darkness. He tried to convince himself that Miss Arvidson expected too much from her students, asking them to do research and then write a theme. Probably the first-string basketball team or the football players would get extra time on such a terrible assignment. They got all the breaks. But none came his way. Nobody cared whether he got his work done or not.

Miss Arvidson is so unfair that she won't give me extra time, and I can't finish this now, so I might as well forget it, he thought.

When Del went to English class the next day, he was sure that most of the kids would be like him and have the theme unfinished. He was surprised to find that he was one of only two or three who were unprepared. Miss Arvidson warned them what was going to happen.

"I've given plenty of time on this theme," she said, and it seemed to Del that she was glaring at him. "So those of you who have failed to get the work done on time are without excuse. If you have done a careless job or failed to hand in a paper, I'm afraid you'll be getting a mid-marking-period warning notice.

She had a lot more to say about it, but Del stopped listening. She had already made it quite clear that he would get a warning notice. Then Danny and Kay would ground him and that would be the end of basketball. But then nobody cared what happened to him anyway.

Still, he thought maybe he could get out of it somehow. For one thing he was counting on a number of students in her other classes being late. Or maybe one of the varsity basketball squad would miss the deadline. If that happened, he felt sure she would have to give an extension to all of them. He wondered, too, if she might not be bluffing. No matter what happened, though, he was determined not to worry about it.

On Monday, however, he was furious. Miss Arvidson did not relent. Del skipped basketball practice that night. He thought it was foolish to practice if he was going to be put off the team when warning notices came out. He stormed home, slammed the front door, and rushed past DeeDee who was sitting in the living room.

"What are you doing here so early?" she asked. "Isn't there any basketball practice tonight?"

"What's it to you?" he demanded. Then he hurried to his room and banged the door shut.

He knew there was no reason to be angry with DeeDee. He was just mad, and she happened to be in the way. He threw his book on the bed and plunked himself into a chair.

Why did everything bad have to happen to him? If Doug or DeeDee were failing in a subject, the whole family would be crowding around trying to help. And if it happened to Doug, the coach would probably assign somebody to help him study so he could get his grade brought up in the shortest amount of time.

But not him! Nobody cared whether he flunked or not. Of course, he hadn't told anyone about it. He was supposed to go in and talk with Miss Arvidson at the earliest opportunity, but what good would that do?

He could hear her now. She could sound so sweet while she said the meanest things. "I'm sorry, Delbert, but you know what I told you at the time I assigned the theme. You've had three weeks to get this theme finished. That's as much time as everyone else has had. There will be no extension of time. You will have to learn that you must meet assignment deadlines." Well, he was not going to go in and see her and let her gloat over him. There was no use in his trying to work it out, anyway. Nothing ever went right for him.

When Kay called everyone to dinner, Del got to his feet slowly. If he had not been so hungry, he would have skipped dinner. But if he did that, he knew Danny would want to know what was wrong. And that was one thing he could do without just then – a lecture on keeping his studies up.

In spite of the fact that DeeDee had her own problems and was becoming increasingly discouraged at trying to work with Letitia, she refused to give up. She spent as much time as she possibly could with her, and Letitia began to open up. The change was not great. It was only a crack in the all-but-impenetrable wall she had built around herself, but it was a crack, nevertheless.

But then one afternoon, all DeeDee had accomplished collapsed. DeeDee was late getting to the lunchroom and most of the other kids had eaten and left. At first, she had not seen Letitia and was not even aware of the fact that she was still there. As she started to sit down, however, she saw a familiar green dress three tables away. It was Letitia sitting alone. Her face was buried in her arms on the table and she appeared to be sobbing silently.

DeeDee hurried over to her. "Letitia," she exclaimed, "what's wrong?"

The other girl did not answer her.

"What's the matter?" She sat down beside her and put her hand on her shoulder.

"Leave me alone," she mumbled. "Just go away and leave me alone."

DeeDee started to leave, but something stopped her. It was as though she had begun to see the anguish in Letitia's heart. She drew her chair closer to the distraught girl.

"I want to help you," she said tenderly. "Please believe me."

Letitia looked up, her tearstained eyes defiant.

"You say that," she blurted almost angrily. "But you don't mean it! You don't care anything about me!"

CHAPTER 9

A SECOND CHANCE

DeeDee rested her hand on Letitia's arm compassionately. Gone was her own irritation at the way the other girl ignored her. Gone for the moment, at least, was her own feeling of loneliness, lost in the greater need of the girl beside her. She could not understand what was troubling Letitia, but she wanted desperately to help her.

DeeDee knew how Letitia felt even though she did not know the reason. She had felt like crying like that many times since they had moved to Rock Point. She had not wanted to have anyone else around, either. Yet, she could not go away and leave Letitia, not when she felt so miserable.

"Is there anything I can do?" she asked quietly. Letitia shook her head.

"I do want to help you. Honestly, I do."

Letitia stopped crying for a moment and she raised her head. "You don't care about me! Nobody does!"

"But I do care," DeeDee protested. Her voice broke and for a moment she was silent. Why was it that words could sound so empty, so inadequate at such a time? She did not even know how to express the turmoil and sympathy that surged within her own heart. "I care and so does God. He loves you and wants to help you, if you'll only let Him."

Letitia raised her head and she looked as though she was about to start crying once more. "You'll never make me believe that," she retorted almost belligerently.

"It doesn't matter what you think. It's true."

"I used to think you liked me," she managed, "but I know now that you just talk that way to try to make me feel good. And that doesn't mean much!" Letitia's voice choked off as she slowly became aware that many other people in the dining room were watching her and DeeDee curiously. She pushed her chair back from the table and stood up. "Sorry, I've got to run." She managed a frail smile.

DeeDee stared helplessly after her as she disappeared out the door and up the hall in the direction of her locker. She had never felt so inadequate or bewildered. There was nothing she could say or do that would ease the pain Letitia was experiencing.

DeeDee was still sitting there, her meal untouched

on the table in front of her, when Tina Nicholson came over and sat down.

"Hi," she said happily. "I've been looking all over for that brother of yours. Have you seen him?"

"Which one?" DeeDee knew Tina was asking about Doug, but she could not resist teasing her.

Tina's cheeks colored delicately. "You know which one. Does Doug have lunch this period today?"

"No, I think he has woodshop or chemistry or something."

"I was afraid of that. I've got to get a message to him, but I haven't been able to find him."

"Can I help?"

"Would you?" I'm supposed to meet him at the snack shop on Wilson Avenue after school, but I'm going to be a little late. I wanted him to know."

"He has a class next to mine this afternoon. I'll tell him."

Tina hesitated. At first it had seemed like a good idea to have DeeDee relay her message. Now, however, she had doubts. He might not like it if she sent a message to him with his sister. She supposed it would be better if she could explain to him that she had to go to the library as soon as school was out that afternoon to get a history book for a special report.

"Would you tell him that I'd like to talk to him for a minute right after school? He can meet me at my locker."

"I'll tell him," DeeDee assured her.

Tina got her food and came to sit with DeeDee. She thought Doug's sister was a nice kid and wished she could get a little better acquainted with her.

DeeDee cut her meat thoughtfully. Already she had practically forgotten about Doug and what she was going to tell him. She could think only of Hank's sister and how sad she was and the way she refused an offer of help and friendship.

"Did you see Letitia just now?" DeeDee asked.

"I certainly did. What was the matter with her?"

DeeDee shrugged. "I don't have a clue."

"Maybe she had a fight with her boyfriend."

"I thought of that, but I don't think she even goes with any boys. She doesn't go with anyone that I know of, at least."

"I guess she doesn't, at that. I really haven't been around her that much."

DeeDee's eyes narrowed. It seemed to her that Tina did not really care about Letitia or helping her. Tina should have gotten to know her in church, young people's group, and Sunday school.

DeeDee saw Doug and told him where to meet Tina after school. He grunted unintelligibly and walked into his class. For a minute or two she was sorry she had even relayed the information. He seemed so unappreciative.

DeeDee did not spend much time thinking about Doug and Tina. She was still so concerned about Letitia that she could think of little else the rest of the day. She could not get the image of Letitia's sad face out of her mind.

If only her distraught, tormented friend would say what was causing her such anguish, there might be something that could be done to help. As it was, she was completely powerless to do anything for her.

DeeDee did not think that she was so wise that she could solve Letitia's problems herself. She had difficulty handling her own problems, and Letitia's seemed a lot worse than anything she had faced.

Still, she knew how much it had meant to Sandy Cole back in Fairview to have someone to share her problems with when her folks got their divorce and her mother remarried. Just being able to talk over those things that hurt her so much seemed to be a big help. She and Sandy had been able to pray together, for one thing. And she knew enough about Sandy's trouble to pray intelligently on her own. As it was, she could only ask God to meet Letitia's need, whatever it was.

DeeDee was still thinking about her friend when they finished dinner that evening and had their family devotions. When the time came for prayer requests she asked Danny to pray for Letitia.

"Certainly, we'll pray for her, DeeDee," he said. "We'll be glad to." He paused. "What is it that we're supposed to pray about?"

She could not answer him at first. Then she said, "I don't know what her problem is, but she is terribly unhappy, she has no friends, and she doesn't seem to want any. I've tried to get close to her, but it seems hopeless." DeeDee dabbed a few tears away from her eyes.

"It's not your fault that Letitia's like that," Del exclaimed. "I wouldn't get so upset over her, if I were you."

"Neither would I," Doug added. "She always has seemed like something of a freak to me."

DeeDee came quickly to Letitia's defense.

"She isn't like that at all. She's a very nice person. The only trouble is that right now she's really bothered by something that she feels is so personal she can't talk it over with anyone."

Danny said that he was glad to see DeeDee so concerned about her friend, whether Letitia seemed to appreciate it or even want her concern and friendship. They all prayed for her that evening and decided to continue to pray for her privately. That made DeeDee feel a little better, but she was still disturbed over Letitia's unhappiness.

Del promised to pray for Letitia, too, and he did so, but he was not too concerned about her. He had other things to think about, like that English theme he had not handed in and the warning notice he was going to get. At first, he was not going to say anything to anyone about it, but he had to have somebody to talk to. Since Doug was the person closest to him, that was who he went to.

"I don't know what I'm going to do, Doug," he began. "The eligibility lists will be coming out in a couple of days. The way things are now I'll never make it. I'll have to turn in my suit."

Doug wasn't so sure that was the only alternative. "Did you ever think about going to Miss Arvidson and talking to her about it?"

"Yeh, she told me to come in for a conference, but a lot of good that would do."

"It might do more good than you think it would. Maybe she'll let you finish your theme now or give you another assignment to make up for the one you missed."

"It's no use." Disgust tinged his voice. "She wouldn't give me a break."

Doug was not ready to accept that. "Come off it, Del," he countered. "You can't make me buy that. You probably just think she's got it in for you. You don't know, she might really want to help you."

"That's a laugh! Just how much help can there be in a blow below the belt like this one?"

"Why don't you try talking to her?"

"I tell you it's just a waste of time."

"If it is, so what? The worst that can happen is that she won't listen to you. And she just might decide to give you another chance."

Del's frown spread across his handsome face. He wanted to think Miss Arvidson would listen to him, but he had already convinced himself that talking to her would be useless.

"That's just what she wants. She'd get a charge out of having me come crawling to her."

Doug shrugged indifferently. There were times when he got more disgusted with his brother than anyone else he knew. And this was one of those times.

"Suit yourself. If you want to flunk English, just let things go. But if I were you and wanted to play any more basketball this year I'd sure go in and talk to her. I wouldn't care whether she got a kick out of having me crawl to her or not."

Del turned from his brother to look out across the snow covered valley at the distant peaks. At first, he was indignant and hurt at Doug's insistence. He expected his brother to understand how much Miss Arvidson had wronged him. He never expected to get so much advice.

But the more he thought about it, the more sensible Doug's idea seemed. Maybe it would do no good at all to talk to Miss Arvidson, but it could not make things any worse.

The following morning Del went directly from his locker to Miss Arvidson's room. She was sitting at her desk when he entered.

"Good morning, Del." Her voice was warm and friendly, just as he thought it would be. She would start out like that. She would probably even be nice when she told him she had already decided to fail him for the quarter. "Is there something I can do for you?"

He cleared his throat and began. There was something about her manner that put him on the defensive. "I came in to talk with you about that theme I should've handed in."

It seemed to him that she stiffened noticeably, but there was no trace of irritation or anger in her voice.

"Yes?"

"I'm sorry I didn't get it in when it was due," he told her. "I see now that I had plenty of time to finish it, but...." How could he tell her that he had failed to hand in his assignment because he was feeling sorry for himself?

"But what?"

"I just fooled around." He blurted out the words. "There wasn't any excuse for it."

"And you would like to have me give you more time, is that it?"

There it was! She was going to tell him that he deserved to fail English. For an instant he wanted to turn around and get out of there. But it was too late for that. He had to go on.

"I'd like to work out something to get my grade up," he told her.

Miss Arvidson riffled thoughtfully through the papers on her desk. It seemed to him as though she was never going to reply.

"Your attitude is considerably different this

morning than it was the day the themes were due, Del. Attitude means a great deal to me."

He stared at her in disbelief. She was actually smiling at him. How about that?

"Do you mean you'll let me work out something so I can get a passing grade in English?" he asked.

"How much of the theme do you have finished?"

"I've got about half the research finished and a little over half the paper written. At least that's what I think is left."

"And how much more time do you think it will take?"

"A week, if I work really hard on it."

"You work extra hard on it and have it finished by next Friday evening after school. Do you think you can do that?"

"I'll sure try!"

"Of course, I won't be able to give you as good a grade on it as I could have if you had handed it in when it was due, but I will accept it and grade it if you want to finish it now."

"Oh, thanks!" he exclaimed. "Thanks a lot!"

He headed toward his homeroom, still stunned by what had taken place. Doug said something like this might happen, but he thought it would be impossible. He thought a conference with Miss Arvidson would be a waste of time. He had surely been wrong about that.

It would not be easy for Del to get the work done

on that theme quickly enough so it could be graded in time for him to make the eligibility list when warning notices were sent out, but that did not matter so much now. He was more interested in getting his grade up to a respectable level because Doug and Miss Arvidson had proven to him that they really cared about him.

Del checked out the books he needed from the library during his study hall, then he rushed right home after practice to write his theme. All weekend long he did research, and then he kept writing until by Thursday he had the theme finished. Miss Arvidson glanced at it quickly.

"It looks as though you did a good job on this, Del," she told him. "I'm glad you tried again."

Still, he stood there.

"I sure want to thank you for giving me another chance on my English grade, Miss Arvidson." He had difficulty speaking. "I really appreciate it."

"That's quite all right. Only see that it doesn't happen again." Her smile took the edge off her words.

CHAPTER 10

STILL A SUB

Once DeeDee started praying for Letitia, her concern for her grew with each passing day. She tried to talk with her at school on several occasions, but she was unable to make progress in improving their relationship. It seemed to her that Hank's sister was determined to keep a certain distance between them.

They met occasionally in the halls. Even in a school the size of theirs they still saw each other once in a while. When it happened, however, Letitia made sure that DeeDee could never approach her alone. She swept by with little more than a stiff, unfriendly nod. She was even colder and more indifferent in the lunchroom where they had met so often before. Her every action made it clear to DeeDee that she wanted to be left alone.

DeeDee was deeply hurt and talked with Kay about it.

"I'd like to have her as a friend and be able to help her if I could," she said, "but she doesn't seem to want my friendship. She acts as though I'm one of those offenders in a bad breath commercial."

Kay looked thoughtful as she stirred the soup she was making. It was difficult to understand why a confused girl like Letitia acted as she did.

"I rather imagine she's feeling embarrassed about letting you see her cry and she wants to keep you from talking about it," Kay advised.

"But why?" DeeDee wanted to know. "I'm her friend. I certainly wouldn't laugh at her."

"I know you wouldn't laugh at her, too, but Letitia isn't sure you wouldn't. To some people it's terribly disturbing for others to know that they have problems."

DeeDee went to the refrigerator and poured herself a glass of milk. At first, she thought Kay was wrong in what she said about Hank's sister. She was sure that Letitia knew she could trust her. At least she should know that by this time. She had not told anyone except her family about Letitia crying in the lunchroom, and she only mentioned it to them so that they could pray about it. She had no other reason for it.

How could it be that Letitia was upset because DeeDee saw her cry? There had been about a hundred other kids in the room too. It was no secret. So there had to be some other reason.

DeeDee could see that she would just have to become better acquainted with Letitia to win her confidence.

"Do you think it would do any good to phone her, Kay?" DeeDee asked.

"It might," Kay said. "If you call her on the phone, she can't very well avoid you."

"She could hang up."

"She could, but I don't think she'd be that rude."

DeeDee knew Kay expected her to go to the phone immediately, but she decided to take time to think and pray about it first.

* * *

Doug continued to make a name for himself on the basketball court. As the season wore on, his place in the squad became even more secure. He still did not make the starting lineup, but he was one of those reliable forwards whose play improved steadily with each passing game. He could go out on the floor when the game was tight and play as calmly as he would if they were thirty points ahead. Yet he had that fierce desire to win. As the final game of the season approached, the coach spent more time with him.

"I'm real glad we've got you, Davis. Your play has meant a lot the last few games. I'm counting on you for Friday night."

Doug tucked the basketball under his arm and eyed the coach quizzically. He was wondering what the coach meant. It hardly seemed possible that he could get to start after spending so much of the early part of the game on the bench. But it could be that he would make the starting lineup. If he did say so himself, he had done all right the last few games. In most schools he would have been on the starting lineup from the first of the season. He was glad enough to be on the first string and able to log a little time in each game.

"Yes," the coach continued, "we have to think about what might happen. Eddie could have an off night or get unlucky and foul out early. We've got to be prepared for whatever might happen."

Doug shifted the ball to his other arm and looked away to hide his sudden embarrassment. He guessed he had learned exactly where he stood as far as making the starting five was concerned. He was still a sub. He must be an important sub according to the way the coach talked, but he was a sub. The realization stunned him.

Oh well, he thought, there was always next year. He would work harder than ever and get in better condition. Then he could do better and would be on the starting five.

He dribbled across the floor. He was competitive enough to be rankled by the fact that he was still on the list of subs, but he was getting to play enough to earn a letter, and that meant a lot to him. He was getting some good experience that would help a lot the following year, so he guessed he had nothing to complain about. Nothing like Del had.

His triplet brother approached the end of the basketball season with the same relaxed attitude he had carried all year. Del was on the second team, and he had no illusions about even getting to suit up with the first squad. He knew he was not good enough. But it made no difference to him. In a way he liked it. He and his teammates did not have the pressure to win that the varsity had, for one thing, and the games were more fun. He found himself liking the sport better all the time.

"I suppose you guys will both be glad when the season's over," Danny said two nights before the last and most important game of the year.

"I'll be glad when the afternoon practices are over," Del said, "but I'll sure miss the games."

Doug looked up in surprise. He had expected Del to just keep quiet or tell Danny that he was glad that the whole thing was over.

"Don't tell me that you're starting to enjoy the game!" Doug exclaimed.

"Well, I am," Del said quietly. "I'm starting to enjoy playing and I don't care anymore which squad I'm on; I just have a great time playing."

Doug grinned because he was beginning to feel the same way too.

* * *

It was several days after DeeDee asked Kay about the wisdom of phoning Letitia that she finally got the courage to do so after she made one last attempt to talk to her in the hall. Since that was unsuccessful, a phone call was the last resort.

She had already decided that if Letitia rebuffed her once more, she was going to give up. She would tell Hank there was nothing she could do for his sister and she was not about to try anymore. She knew that would upset him, but it was useless to try to keep working with someone who was totally unresponsive.

After praying briefly, DeeDee took the phone from the cradle and dialed the number. Mrs. Warren answered, her voice thin and whining.

"I don't know whether Letitia is in her room or not," she said, a certain reluctance creeping into her tone. "I'll see."

DeeDee put her hand over the mouthpiece. "It's working, Kay," she whispered. "Her mother's calling her now."

But Letitia did not come to the phone. DeeDee could hear them talking about it angrily. Her mother tried to persuade her to come and talk and Letitia was just as firm in her determination not to. After two or three minutes Mrs. Warren returned.

"I'm sorry, but Letitia doesn't feel very well," she said apologetically. "She would rather not come to the phone right now."

"Oh, I'm sorry." DeeDee had not intended to question Mrs. Warren, but the words popped out. "Is she very ill?"

"Well, I–I'll have her phone you after a while,"

Mrs. Warren muttered. "Could you leave your name and phone number, please?"

DeeDee gave her the information, numbly. She was not fooled. She had heard Letitia almost shouting that she was not about to come to the phone to talk to anybody.

It was no use, DeeDee told herself. The other girl was determined not to talk to her. Nothing she could do would change her.

DeeDee was sure Letitia would not return her phone call. In that, she was not disappointed. Although she was studying until 10:30 p.m., there was no telephone call for her. She would not have mentioned it but Kay asked her about it.

"Maybe she forgot," Kay said hopefully.

DeeDee did not reply. However, she was not ready to accept such an easy explanation. No one could make her believe that her friend had forgotten. There was only one reason she refused to return the call. She simply did not want to talk to DeeDee.

DeeDee wondered why she had even wanted to try to help Letitia. She was going to have to tell Hank that she had been a dismal failure.

Choking back the tears, DeeDee went to her room. Before going to bed that night she wrote to Sandy Cole back in Fairview, telling her how much she missed the school and all her old friends. Her homesickness was just as bad then as it had been when they first moved, and DeeDee had no idea how to get over it.

CHAPTER 11

ENCOURAGEMENT

As the night of the final basketball game of the season drew near, excitement raced through the school. It had not reached the intensity of feeling and spirit that was always felt at Fairview. DeeDee thought there would never be as much interest in sports at Northwest as they had had in their former school. But the season had been good and the feeling was high.

After two early season losses that in recent weeks had been all but forgotten, Enders had rolled unbeaten over their opposition. They sewed up the conference title three weeks before and were picked by the experts to have an easy time of putting down Rock Point's Northwest High.

Many of the followers of the school's athletic teams were ready to write off the game, but the team was determined to go down fighting. At a pep rally in the afternoon of the game, the coach sounded the battle cry that sent the team racing out onto the floor determined to show everyone they were not whipped yet.

"We all know what the sports writers have been saying," the coach began. "They're telling the world that we don't have a chance against Enders tonight, but we're not willing to hand them the victory. We're going out there and knock off the giant. We'll show those so-called experts that they don't know what they're talking about."

He went on to outline the long years of rivalry between the two schools and how often the favorite had been knocked off. He called attention to the football season and the baseball game the previous spring. Northwest had been beaten both times.

"That's why everyone thinks they're so much better than we are," he went on, pausing to let his gaze wander over the crowd. "And I don't like that. I don't like it at all."

The kids were beginning to believe the basketball team had a chance. That was apparent in the way they sat erect, cheering at every encouraging phrase. "We've got a chance to redeem ourselves tonight. If we can win this game, we'll show everyone that Enders can't assume they're going to win whenever they play Northwest High." The crowd roared with enthusiasm at the coach's words.

When he finished, two of the starting five spoke

briefly, pledging themselves to play their best. They, too, were confident that they could win, and were going to win. By the time the pep rally was over the student body was behind the basketball team more than they had been all year.

Changing into his uniform for the game that night, Doug was tense. Sweat left a clammy film on his lean face and the palms of his hands, and fear and excitement tightened about his chest until his breathing was quick and shallow. He hoped the other guys would not see that his fingers trembled. After all, he was only a sub. He might not even get to play. There was nothing for him to be so shook up about. But it was worse than it had been at any other game all season, even when he was moved up to the first string and had had to prove himself.

Waiting for the game to begin, he wondered what it must be like for the guys who were going to start. The chances were that they would feel a lot more uptight than he did.

From the opening jump ball, the game took off at a furious pace. Enders got the tip and raced down the court for an effortless layup that put them on the scoreboard first, 2-0.

Northwest got possession of the ball under their own basket and moved it deliberately across the center line. They were moving slower than Enders, but with a taut expectancy, as though they were ready to explode on signal.

Eddie, the man Doug usually substituted for, took the ball from the center on a short, rifled pass, dribbled toward the basket and sank a long one-handed shot. Moments later he stole the ball from their startled guard and fired it across the court to the other forward who was moving in fast. Seconds later Northwest had tied the score and forged ahead.

All through the first quarter the lead moved back and forth during the hard-fought battle. Then, early in the second period Eddie went out on fouls. A groan went up from the crowd. After all, he had scored more than half of Northwest's points and was easily the star of the game so far.

Doug went out on the floor under difficult circumstances. He would have to play better than he had ever played in his life just to look as good as the one he replaced. He was so nervous he flubbed the first pass to him and Enders took the ball. Then he settled down enough to steal the basketball and set up another two-pointer. A roar of approval went up from the crowd.

That play set the pace of the rest of the game for Doug. He was all over the court on both offense and defense, fighting Enders savagely. The crowd was on its feet and the gym roared with excitement as the final seconds ticked off.

Northwest was ahead by a single point, and it looked as though the victory was theirs. But then the opposing center snatched the ball from Northwest and fired it half across the court to a forward driving hard toward the goal. Doug threw himself into the air in a desperate attempt to deflect the ball, but it skimmed past, just beyond the tips of his fingers. It hit the backboard and angled downward through the hoop as the final gun sounded.

Northwest was beaten!

The full realization of the catastrophe brought by the goal that swished through the net an eyelash before the final gun sounded came slowly to the Northwest five. They had been playing so hard and so confidently that they found it difficult to accept defeat.

But the last game of the season was over. People were pouring out of the bleachers and surging onto the floor on their way to the exits. The Northwest fans, so noisy a few moments before, were silent now, their voices stilled by a skillful shot from beneath the basket. Numbly the players looked about, beginning to accept the fact that victory had been snatched from them even as the game ended.

Doug made his way to the locker room. As he pushed quietly through the crowd, he was glad that nobody said anything to him. He certainly did not feel like talking right then. The sting of defeat was still hurting him. As far as he was concerned, it was not enough that he had played the best game of his life, or that Northwest had pushed Enders harder than anyone had ever pushed them since their losses early in the season.

Nor did it mean anything to him now that Northwest had been ahead throughout the entire fourth quarter, except for the goal Enders sank in the final two seconds of play. They had lost. That was all that mattered. Doug was not sure how the other players felt, but nothing short of victory could have given him any satisfaction.

Doug showered and dressed as quickly as possible. He wanted to avoid talking to the coach and the other team members. He would have avoided talking to Tina, too, if she had not been outside waiting for him. He had asked her to go out with him for a sundae. He put on his coat and was just leaving the locker room when Eddie called out to him.

"Wait a second, Doug. I'll take you home."

He stopped at the door, reluctantly. "Thanks, some other time. I've got a date."

"I'd like to talk to you for a minute. I just wanted to tell you that you played a great game tonight."

Doug ignored the compliment. "Thanks, Eddie, but I've got to run. I've got plans."

The other boy's laughter rang throughout the locker room. "Plans? What you really mean is that you've got Tina Nicholson waiting outside for you."

Someone else broke in good naturedly. "We don't blame you for turning down Eddie's wheels for her old man's Cadillac. We would, too, if we had the chance. So would Eddie."

"Lay off, will you?"

"Think she'll be waiting for you? Maybe one of those Enders hotshots has got her lined up now."

Doug realized how red his face was becoming, so he hurried to the door as quickly as he could.

The coach called to him. "Just a minute, Davis. I want to talk to you."

He turned around and came back, reluctantly.

"You played a good game tonight. I was proud of you."

"But we lost," Doug put in disappointedly.

"I know, and I feel as badly about that as you do, but I wanted you to know that you played a good game. You gave us everything you had."

Doug's gaze came up to meet that of the coach's.

"Thanks, Coach, I appreciate your encouragement," he said.

"And don't let that gal keep you out too late tonight," he added. "Remember that you're still in training."

Doug managed a slight grin and then he hurried out of the locker room.

What the coach said made Doug feel good in spite of the fact that they had been beaten. As far as the other guys' teasing him was concerned, he could take that. Tina was a great gal and prettier than any other girl in school. Any of the guys would be excited about a chance to go out with her, that was sure.

The closing door shut out the laughter, and he crossed the hall to the place where she was waiting for him. He hoped she had not heard what the guys were saying. He would not want her to be hurt because they were too stupid to keep their mouths shut.

When he reached her, however, she was as cheery as ever. Doug was relieved.

"Hi," she said when she saw him. Her voice was bright and joyful, irritating him briefly with her lack of understanding. He could not comprehend how she could be as happy as she appeared to be if she knew that they had lost.

"I didn't mean to keep you waiting," he told her.

They started off together and, as usual, she started to chatter about the game. "I was so proud of you tonight, Doug. Everybody said you were great. And you really did play a good game."

"I'll say I was great." Sarcasm honed his words. "Or didn't you see what happened? My man scored the winning basket. I played a tremendous game."

She defended him loyally. "But that wasn't your fault. If it hadn't been for the way you guarded him, we wouldn't even have been close. You held him as well as Eddie did when he was in. Maybe even better."

It made Doug feel good to know that she found excuses for him, but it was irritating, too. How could she be that way? Did she care at all that they had been beaten after they had the game won? If all girls were like that it was no wonder that Northwest had not won the conference basketball trophy. Tina certainly did not care enough about winning to satisfy him.

The morning after Letitia refused to talk to DeeDee on the phone, DeeDee still felt as bad as she had the night before. It seemed that everything had come unraveled. She would have stayed home from school that day, but she knew Kay would never accept that as an excuse.

DeeDee went to school at the usual time that morning even though she felt unhappy and almost ill from the restless night she had spent. As she stood at her locker, sorting out the books she needed for her morning classes, Letitia came around the corner.

"Oh, DeeDee!" she exclaimed when she saw her. "There you are!"

"Hi," she answered. DeeDee was so surprised she could hardly speak. Besides, there was a limit to what she could take from one person and she had had enough.

"I've been looking for you," Letitia explained.

"I just got here." That was a stupid remark, she told herself. Anyone could see that she had just arrived. She had not even taken off her coat yet.

The hurt still apparent in her every move, DeeDee faced her locker and put her books on the upper shelf. Although she did not look around, she knew that Letitia was still at her elbow.

"I'm sorry I didn't phone you last night," she said apologetically.

"That's all right. I didn't have anything very important to talk to you about, anyway."

"It was rude of me not to call you back. I really don't have any excuse for it. But I am sorry."

DeeDee could not keep from smiling. "That's all right," she repeated. She had abandoned all hope that Letitia would change. It was good to know that she had been wrong.

They walked down the corridor to the next wing where they both had their homerooms. They talked about insignificant things, but DeeDee was encouraged. It was not until they reached Letitia's homeroom, however, that she finally said what was on her mind.

"I'm so glad that you're not mad at me. I worried so much about it last night that I could hardly sleep. I thought about getting up and calling you, but I was afraid that you'd be asleep and I didn't want to waken you."

"Don't think any more about it. I'm not going to," DeeDee said. And she meant it. It was enough for her to know that Letitia really did want to be friends with her. "How about having lunch with me this noon?" she asked.

Letitia blushed and said timidly, "I didn't know whether you'd even want to talk to me again after what happened in the lunchroom the other day. I have never been so embarrassed in my life."

"You shouldn't be. I felt so sorry for you I could have cried myself."

Embarrassment tinged the lobes of Letitia's ears and crept down into her neck. "I don't know what was the matter with me," she went on. "I don't usually cry very often, but that day everything piled so high I thought I couldn't stand it anymore."

"I know." DeeDee was understanding. "Maybe we can talk more about it at noon."

The other girl jerked erect. "There's nothing more to talk about."

"Well, that's good. I was afraid you might have some serious problems."

"I don't know what would ever give you that idea," Letitia said defensively. She looked up at the clock on the wall. "Sorry, but I've got to run. I'll see you at noon."

Suddenly DeeDee felt the load she had been carrying loosen and slip away.

In the days that followed Letitia and DeeDee made progress in their friendship. Letitia still seemed to lack trust in others, but she did seem to enjoy DeeDee's company. They ate together when they had lunch at the same time, and occasionally, Tina or some of the other girls would join them. It was not long before they were walking home together after school and sitting together in church.

Kay noticed how their friendship had developed.

"We get along great together now," DeeDee told her.

"That's wonderful. Danny and I have been praying about it. We knew how disturbed you were."

"Thanks. Prayer was what this situation needed all along; it just took me a while to realize it."

"There's something else I've been wanting to ask you, DeeDee. I've been watching you the last couple of weeks. You act more like yourself than you have at any time since we moved out here from Minnesota."

DeeDee hesitated. She had not thought about it, but now that Kay mentioned it, she had to admit that was true. She had no more friends than before. In fact, Letitia was about the only one, except for Tina, and she was with Doug most of the time.

"I hadn't actually thought about it before," DeeDee said, "but I have felt more relaxed and happier recently."

"I'm glad. We've been praying about that, too."

DeeDee was amazed at what had happened. The circumstances were much the same. She was still as far away from her old friends as ever and she had very few new friends. But things were different. She no longer had that icy emptiness inside. Nor did she feel like crying all the time. She explained to Kay how she felt.

"I think you've learned something that's very important," her foster mother told her. "And something that a lot of people never learn in an entire lifetime. You can wipe out your own unhappiness by getting your attention off yourself and onto God and other people." She paused for a moment. "You started thinking about Letitia and trying so hard to help her that your attitude toward your own troubles changed. You no longer gave them preeminence."

DeeDee realized it was true. She was still lonely, but her attitude toward her loneliness had changed.

"But I haven't been able to help Letitia all that much," she said somberly. "In most ways I don't think I've been able to help her at all."

"Maybe you haven't yet, but your problem of loneliness has been solved. God will work in her life, too, in time. We have only to keep on praying and trust the Lord to work in His way."

When DeeDee went into her room she was humming a little tune. It was strange how much nicer Rock Point and the school had suddenly become. She knew she was going to make friends. It might take a little more time than it had taken when they were first in Fairview, but it would happen. She was convinced of it. Although she still missed Sandy and the others, she was able to thank God that He had led them to Colorado and Northwest High. It was exciting to see what opportunities would open up for each of them. And now DeeDee could look forward to an answer to Letitia's problem, not because she had found a solution, but because she was going to trust the Lord to solve it.

THE DANNY ORLIS SERIES

The Danny Orlis series, by Bernard Palmer, delivers a blend of adventure, mystery, and suspense through various settings—from the Canadian wilderness to Guatemalan jungles. Danny Orlis, an adept outdoorsman, skilled athlete, and committed Christian, employs his quick thinking, calm bravery, and biblical solutions to confront everyday problems and hair-raising dangers. Early stories focus on Danny navigating school life, sports, and outdoor challenges, while in later books, Danny and his wife Kay provide wisdom and guidance to youngsters facing lifelike situations and challenges. Having sold over two million copies, this series has made Palmer a renowned author in Christian youth literature. Palmer is also the author of the Felicia Cartright series and various other series for Christian youth.

AVAILABLE FROM WWW.ANEKOPRESS.COM

www.ingramcontent.com/pod-product-compliance
Lightning Source LLC
Chambersburg PA
CBHW060503300726

48975CB00008B/2624